Fanny
and
Victorian Jack

By
Lynne D.M. Noble

Shield Crest

© Copyright 2018 Lynne D.M. Noble

All rights reserved

ISBN: 978-1-912505-13-5
First Edition

A CIP catalogue record for this book
is available from the British Library

MMXVIII

Published by

ShieldCrest Publishing Limited
Aylesbury, Buckinghamshire, HP18 0TF
England.

www.shieldcrest.co.uk

Dedication

This book is dedicated to Jack and Liam Wilby,
who inspired me to write it.

The illustrator

Michael Hutchinson, the author's husband, is a retired architect and landscape architect and therefore accustomed to preparing design drawings. However, this is the first book which Michael has illustrated and he has enjoyed helping to providing the visual detail which helps to bring the story to life. Together, he and Lynne live in Holmfirth in West Yorkshire, where they retired to in 2009.

Acknowledgement

IT Support – Mike Ptycia

Many thanks to Mike for continuing to keep us sane with all things IT.

Contents

Introduction

Fanny is a little girl with Asperger's Syndrome who lives with her mother, father and brother in a town in Yorkshire. Fanny does not like scrambled egg or the feel of chalk on her fingers. She is brilliant at reading and curious about everything around her but when she is anxious she wraps herself up, very tightly, in her quilt to block out everything. Fanny's mother doesn't really like her being around but this doesn't matter too much to Fanny, who prefers to spend her time lying on the daisy patch on the lawn. There she can watch all the insect activity going on around her.

One day while she is sitting on the daisy patch, Jack appears. Jack is a chimney-sweep and lives in Soho, London. He has been transported to the 1950's by the 'Old Man in the Sky' to help Fanny understand how childhood has changed dramatically in just one hundred years.

Fanny did not realise that many Victorian children did not even live to be five years old in the city slums. From the age of four – if they did survive - children would be forced to sweep chimneys, work in factories and undertake other menial jobs for many hours at a time, just in order to survive. They did not go to school. The Victorian poor often did not have shoes to wear and only had meat to eat on a Sunday.

Fanny desperately wants to help Jack and his family find a way out of the poverty they are in. Hesitatingly, she begins to explore what she can do to help but not before tragedy strikes Jack's family. Fanny finds that it is the things that we often throw away that become the most useful in helping Jack and his family. Along the way, Fanny finds herself transported into the slums of London and she learns first-hand about the reality of life for the Victorian Poor.

This is the first book in a series written about Fanny and Victorian Jack and their travels through Victorian England, and describes many of the changes occurring at that time amid the hardships that were prevalent.

It can be read alone by older readers, providing insight into an age which is very different from ours. It is useful for adding understanding to school projects on this era. Younger readers may like to read this with a parent or guardian as it is written to aid discussion and increase a child's understanding of how the past affects the age we are now living in. The story is intended to extend and develop a child's vocabulary.

Finally, the story is designed to raise awareness of some of the challenges of living with Asperger's Syndrome.

Chapter One

Ever since Fanny had been able to crawl and poke a stick under a rockery stone in her garden, she had been fascinated by the tiny pearly pink bodies that tumbled out, wriggling furiously as they did so. Another prod with her twig revealed a grey and scaly and plumper body that stumbled after them rather crossly before rolling over and lying helplessly on its back. Fanny leaned over, held securely in the rounded hollow of the largest rockery stone, peering at the floundering body. She gently trailed her twig in the soil, in and amongst the insects, but she didn't hurt them. Then she carefully helped the biggest one to roll over so that it could scramble away to safety.

So intent was Fanny on observing her new playmates that she didn't immediately notice the shadow which crept softly over her space.

`Those are woodlice, Fanny!' The voice was gentle and kind, like a soft cloud. `Those pink ones are the ones and that big grey one is the parent.'

Fanny looked at her daddy under her fringe, her startling blue eyes gazing intently at his face. `What do they do?' she asked, moving slightly so that her daddy could sit beside her. He carefully folded his long body so that he could perch beside her without injuring any of woodlice. He smelled of newly mown grass and tomato plants and

1

Fanny snuggled into the coarse woollen waistcoat that he so often wore when he was out in the garden.

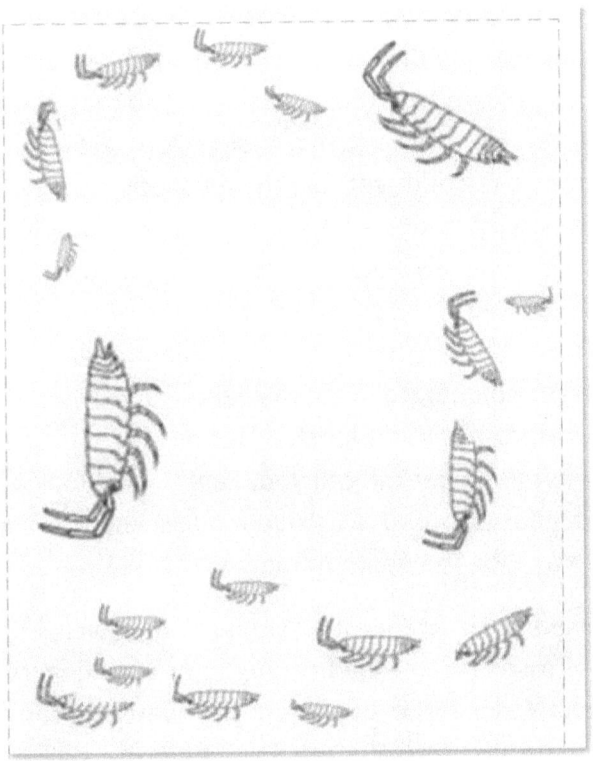

'Sometimes woodlice are called slaters,' Fanny's daddy began. 'They like to hide in dark damp places such as under logs and stones during the day. At night they start searching for food. They like to eat rotting plants – that's why there are so many on the compost heap. They are very useful!'

Fanny smiled at her Daddy. He didn't mind that her nails were ingrained with soil and that her legs were streaked with mud. He didn't mind that that she had clambered up the rockery to perch on the highest stone so that she could investigate all the activity going on around her. Sometimes she could get lost in this world that nobody else seemed to notice - where fat-bodied bumble bees clambered clumsily over harebells and harvestmen spiders picked their way quickly through the undergrowth. Fanny had even been so enthralled when a spider was spinning a web that she hadn't heard her mother calling her in for lunch. Her mother had scolded her, 'Didn't you hear me call you, Fanny? Just look at the state of you! Go and scrub your nails and wash your hands. You'll be the death of me.'

Fanny liked the fragrance of the pink soap, which smelled faintly of roses. It squished through her dirty fingers and when she turned the water on she watched the pale brown foam flop into the pristine sink. She swilled the water round and round, trying to get rid of it, but the water swirled and disappeared, leaving the foam sitting on top of the plughole.

'Fanny, have you finished washing your hands, yet?'

Fanny prodded once more at the foam which stubbornly refused to go down the plughole. She reached for the towel and wiped her fingers quickly. Some of the foam had

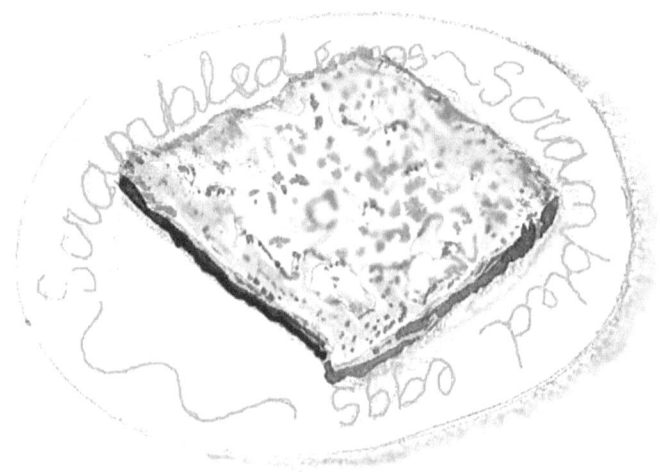

been transferred to the towel, so she turned it over before tossing it back onto the rail. She didn't want to be scolded again.

The table was laid neatly, with a plate of scrambled eggs on toast on each mat. Fanny didn't like scrambled eggs, which for her were yellow and white flecked lumpy bits. It didn't taste of much either but it was much worse when it was served on toast. No matter how much Fanny tried, she couldn't quite manage to cut the toast with her knife and fork and in her efforts she generally managed to spill the scrambled egg over the tablecloth. She waited until her mother had returned to the kitchen and then quickly slipped the toast into her pocket before scooping up the egg onto her fork and swallowing it quickly. Tilly the hamster would like the toast and Fanny's mother wouldn't know any different. Fanny was pleased that her Daddy had allowed her to have a hamster, and Tilly seemed to enjoy everything that Fanny did not like, stuffing all the morsels that Fanny fed her into her pouches. Later, Tilly would briskly stroke her overstuffed cheeks so that the store of food tumbled out of her mouth, then she would delicately pick up a titbit between her delicate paws and nibble contentedly.

Tilly used to live in the house but she had been banned to living in a cage in the garage after she had escaped one evening. Fanny's mother had woken up in the middle of the night to find Tilly busily making a nest in her hair. This had ruined her hairdo and made her quite cross, especially as she had an important appointment the next day. Fanny's mother spent a long time in the bathroom washing and combing her hair the next morning after Daddy had gone to work before eventually leaving for her appointment. Fanny did not dare tell her mother that she had left a bit of hamster poo in her hair. She didn't want to be scolded again.

The following morning after her older brother had gone to school, Fanny was still sitting at the breakfast table swinging her legs and with her socks crumpled around her ankles. She had enjoyed her bowl of cornflakes and Hovis bread slice spread with marmalade but she always took the crusts off the bread and laid them around and under the rim of the plate. They didn't taste the same as the softer bread and because she wore a different dress that didn't have pockets, she couldn't hide the crusts and take them to Tilly either.

Fanny's mother appeared from the kitchen, drying her hands on her apron. 'Well, have you finished?' She demanded.

Fanny nodded.

'Well, go off and play then and mind you don't get dirty or scuff your shoes.'

Fanny slid off the chair and ran outside. Daddy was going to cut the grass tomorrow so she did not have much time to lie in the bed of daisies before their heads would be cut off and tossed through the air before landing silently and desolately on the lawn. Then the bees and harvestman and lumbering beetles with their heavy shiny black armour would temporarily disappear until the grass had grown and the daisies had reappeared.

The dew was still evident in the damp coolness on Fanny's legs as she sat in the middle of the daisy patch before lying down in it. Some clover and one or two buttercups had also sprung up. Fanny lay enveloped in their softness, resisting the urge to scratch her leg where a harvestman spider had dared to scramble over. The cerulean sky was dotted with puffs of white cloud changing form from dragons to angels or the 'old man of the sky' who was in a story which had been read to her at bedtime. The old man of the sky was very old with a whiskery face and benevolent smile. He liked all living things and took care of them. He lived in the sky because he could see all the world from up there and that made his job easier. Fanny raised her hand and waved to him. The cloud changed form and the 'old man of the sky' smiled back before fragmenting and disappearing.

Fanny loved the music surrounding her as she lay in the daisy patch. The birds twittered and warbled, the bees hummed happily and the breeze whispered gently as her hands carelessly wended their way through the blades of grass.

She didn't hear Jack approach and lie down beside her. She never did, but he always appeared when she was alone and he was a good companion to have. He was interesting and although he was about nine – not much older than Fanny – he had never been to school and lived with his seven brothers and sisters in one room in a place called Soho in Victorian Britain.

Jack was a chimney sweep. It was a filthy, dirty job, he told Fanny, but small boys could do this job better than adults. The chimneys were very narrow - sometimes only 30cm – and were twisted, so small boys were sent scrambling up the inside of the chimney to scrape the soot away. Jack's knees and elbows, like those of any other chimney sweep, were always bleeding and sore. Sometimes the Sweep Master would dab some salt water on the wounds but that never stopped him sending Jack or the other boys up another chimney.

Jack had told Fanny about a friend that he'd once had, called Alfie. Alfie had been six and was terrified of the dark. On more than one occasion the Master Chimney Sweep had lit a fire to encourage Alfie to hurry and get a move on cleaning the chimney. But one day, Alfie had got stuck up a very narrow, twisted chimney and suffocated. The Master Sweep had pulled Alfie's lifeless body out of the chimney himself, though the look of terror was still etched on Alfie's face.

Fanny had found it difficult to believe that small boys could be sent up a chimney.

'Didn't anybody try to help the children?' Fanny had asked in all innocence.

Jack nodded wryly. There was an Act passed in 1840 forbidding anyone under the age of 21 from working as chimney sweeps. It was called the Chimney Sweepers and Chimneys Regulation Act but nobody took any notice of it. Why should they? The fine was too small to worry about if the law was ignored and the Master Sweepers still made enough money even if they had to pay a fine.

Fanny had once asked her mother where Victorian Britain was. Her mother had smiled and said, 'That's an odd little question that you've just asked.' Then, with a slightly amused expression on her face, her mother had returned to washing the clothes in the sink before shaking her head slightly.

Fanny had waited until her Daddy came home before asking him about Victorian Britain and he had explained that this was a different time when Queen Victoria was on the throne.

'Didn't children go to school?' Fanny asked her Daddy. She didn't mention Jack because nobody else could see Jack and she was often in enough trouble with her mother for inventing things.

'Children from poor families didn't go to school,' her Daddy explained, 'only children from rich families went to school or had governesses to help them with their studies at home. Children of the Victorian poor might go out to work when they were only five or six to help with paying the bills and the jobs which they did were often very dirty and dangerous.'

'Five or six!' Fanny exclaimed, 'Why, that's younger than me!'

Fanny's Daddy smiled. 'Yes, poppet, that's younger than you are, but they had to help pay the bills. The children often didn't have enough food to eat or clothes to wear and the homes that they lived in were often cold and damp. They were raggedy and thin. There were lots of diseases then and many of the children died. If their parents died they often had to live out on the streets.'

'Why didn't they have some medicine to make them better?' Fanny asked.

'Poor Victorian families couldn't afford medicine. What they really needed was good food, warm clothing and a dry warm house to live in. That would have helped but there wasn't a lot of effective medicine about, anyway. Diseases like measles, scarlet fever, whooping cough and mumps were often fatal. Children weren't protected because immunisation hadn't been discovered then. A lot of children got rickets...'

'Rickets? Fanny responded.

'Yes, rickets! It's a disease which can be prevented by a good diet and sunshine, but the poor Victorian children had a very poor diet and lived in a smoky, murky environment so that the sun's rays could not reach and bathe their skin. Rickets causes the bones to become soft and deformed so their legs were weak and bent and the children's growth was often stunted so that they didn't grow very tall.'

Fanny's daddy stopped momentarily before sighing and ruffling her hair fondly. Then he strode away towards the house. Fanny waited until he had disappeared before making her way to the daisy patch. Jack was still there, lying in the grass, his shoeless feet streaked with soot and the filth of the streets of Soho. Soot also streaked his face and spattered his ragged clothing which hung loosely over his thin frame.

'Can you read, Jack?' Fanny asked him before flopping down beside him.

Jack shook his head, softly.

Fanny didn't know what to say. This was beyond her experience and understanding.

'Are you hungry then?'

Jack nodded his head vigorously so that flakes of soot span into the air and hovered briefly before settling silently on her daisy patch.

'I'll get you something to eat then,' said Fanny with more conviction than she felt. She didn't know how she was going to keep that promise, since she could see her mother was busy in the kitchen and so there wasn't any access to the pantry. Fanny tiptoed to the dustbin and lifted the lid up without making a sound. The bread crusts she had left under her plate had been tipped into a plastic bag so that the mice couldn't get them. Fanny lifted the bag out and ran back up to Jack, dropping the crusts of bread into his lap. He hoisted the bag of crusts up to eye level, looking hungrily at them as he did so. He looked sickly and fragile, with his blackened skin accentuating the hollowed cheeks.

A bee caught Fanny's eye momentarily. When she looked back, Jack had vanished with only the imprint of his body in the daisy patch and a few straying flakes of soot to show that he had been there. Nevertheless, Fanny decided that she would save up all the food that she didn't like for Jack, instead of Tilly, from now on. After all, Tilly always had plenty to eat and Jack didn't and Jack would be back soon. He always was.

1838 Early Victorian shilling coin

Chapter Two

Jack did not appear for a few days after that. This didn't unduly worry Fanny for Jack just appeared whenever Fanny was alone and often there would be someone around 'keeping an eye on Fanny.' Jack had never appeared in the house or at school so Fanny had to be in the garden somewhere on a day when it wasn't raining. That didn't happen very often unless she had been ill like last week when she'd had a sore throat and couldn't go to school.

'This is really inconvenient,' her mother had muttered as though Fanny could have helped being ill. When her daddy had arrived home though, he had bought Lucozade, a colouring book on insects and some crayons for her.

Today though was Saturday. Fanny's mother was going to the market and didn't want the 'encumbrance of a child' when she did so. Fanny didn't mind being an encumbrance if it meant she could be near her daddy or that Jack would come. She hoped that she would always be an encumbrance, so Fanny skipped happily to the daisy patch while her daddy attended to the car tyre which had apparently burst.

Jack was already waiting for her when she flopped down onto the lawn. He was still wearing the same clothes which were now even dirtier and smellier than Fanny could remember. He smelt like a stinky toilet that Fanny's mother had refused to use when they had been on holiday but Fanny was too polite to tell him so.   Jack's face was still blackened with soot so that only the whites of his eyes could be seen.

'What have you been doing, Jack?' Fanny asked as she took some broken biscuit and a potato out of her pocket to hand to him.

Jack took them off her. 'What's this?' he asked, sniffing at the biscuit.

`It's a Jammy Dodger,' Fanny replied, 'I'm sorry it's broken.'

Jack took half of it and slid it into his mouth before closing it and chewing contentedly. A look of pure delight crossed his face. 'That is so good, he commented, 'I've never had anything like that before.'

Fanny smiled. `Eat the rest then,' she urged. Fanny could see the hunger in his eyes but he reluctantly returned the morsel back into his pocket. `Maria's ill. This will be good medicine for her. I'll take it back for her.'

'Who's Maria?' Fanny asked.

`Maria's my sister', Jack replied, 'She's only two and she's really sick.'

'Has she got some Lucozade?'

'Lucozade?' Jack asked, 'What's that?'

'It's golden and fizzy and it's guaranteed to make you feel better when you are ill,' Fanny replied, reeling off her mother's words. 'There's a little bit left in the bottle and my mother is out so I can get you it.' Fanny dashed to the house. She could still hear her daddy moving about in the garage so it was easy to get hold of the Lucozade and just for good measure a couple of slices of corned beef and an onion from the refrigerator, too.

Jack's eyes gleamed when he saw what Fanny had brought him. 'This'll make a really good stew for us all,' he said, fingering the onion, the beef and then the potato as he dropped them into his pocket. `Twill be a lot better than gruel anyway.'

Jack and Fanny sat contentedly in the daisy patch. The golden sun bathed them in soporific warmth until Fanny's eyelids closed, her limbs became heavy and she sank into the cool fresh grass beneath her. The bees hummed a lullaby. She felt like warm syrup oozing into something that she didn't quite understand but when she had tried explaining something similar to her Granddad, he had smiled knowingly and called it 'the peace that passeth all understanding.'

Fanny could hear her mother in the distance, calling her after returning from the market. Fanny hoisted herself up onto her elbow and turned back to where Jack had been laying but he had disappeared again before she could ask him what gruel was. She didn't really know how one onion, one potato and two slices of corned beef could feed seven children and two adults either, but Jack seemed to think it would.

Fanny could hear her mother calling her daddy. 'Harry, have you seen the corned beef we were going to have for lunch?'

'No dear.' Fanny's daddy replied, 'I've only just finished fixing this tyre!'

'Well, I thought it was in the 'fridge,' Fanny's mother muttered, 'perhaps I'm mistaken' and she shook her head slightly and marched back indoors before adding, 'well, it will just have to be scrambled eggs on toast again.' She made it sound like a threat but really, there was no other way to describe scrambled eggs.

When Fanny's mother was safely inside the house, Fanny picked her way carefully down the side of the greenhouse and through the back door of the garage. Her daddy was wiping the oil off his fingers with a rough cloth and his fingers were tinged olive green with the lube.

'Daddy, what's gruel?' Fanny asked, absentmindedly wiping some soot off her fingers onto her dress.

Fanny's daddy squatted down so that his gaze was on a level with hers. 'It's like really thin, watery porridge – not very nice and no golden syrup to make it taste better.' He smiled before ruffling her hair fondly. He was always doing that and Fanny didn't mind at all, even if her ribbons came loose at the same time, but she didn't allow anyone else to do it. No, nobody else at all.

Fanny smiled at her daddy. She didn't think gruel could taste any worse than scrambled eggs but she kept that thought in her head in case her mother heard and she was told that she was an 'ungrateful child.' She kept a lot of thoughts in her head although sometimes they escaped out of her mouth when it was wise not to do so. Sometimes they appeared to amuse her mother but more often than not they earned Fanny an early night in bed so that her mother could get some peace from her.

Fanny wiped the remaining soot off her fingers onto her dress. It was Saturday and Saturday night was bath night. Next time she saw Jack, she must remember to ask him when he had a bath and washed his clothes. It didn't appear to be all that important to him.

'Fanny!' Her mother's voice was more strident and insistent now.

'Better get in now before your mother gets even more upset,' Fanny's daddy advised.

Fanny skipped down the narrow path. Her curls had nearly escaped her ribbons which dangled precariously down her back. Fanny's mother looked in disbelief as her daughter stood there innocently, thumb in mouth, peppered in soot and smeared in grass stains.

'Just what have you done to yourself?' Fanny's mother exclaimed. 'And what is this soot on your dress and..... ugh! .... you smell like a latrine.' She raised her hand ready to strike, but Fanny's daddy was strolling down the narrow garden path, whistling *Somewhere Over the Rainbow*. Fanny's mother thought better of it, dropped her hand and gathering up her skirt, flounced inside.

Fanny did not dare ask what a latrine was.

Chapter Three

It wasn't long before Fanny saw Jack because he appeared next day when she was investigating an earwig which had crept into one of her daddy's prized dahlias. The more that she prodded the insect with a stem of grass the more it inched its way further into the petals. It would eat holes in them, her daddy had once told her. Fanny decided from that point that she didn't like earwigs any more. When she had turned to tell her daddy, she found Jack sitting in the daisy patch, leaning back, with his arms behind him and his mousy hair flopping across his brow.

'How's Maria?' Fanny asked politely, remembering her manners.

'Ain't no better,' Jack replied softly, 'but she liked the Lucozade and Jammy Dodger.'

Fanny didn't know what to say to this. ` I had a bath last night,' she said. 'When is your bath night, Jack?'

Jack leaned backwards on his haunches even more. 'You don't know much, Fanny, do you? It's not like it is here, you know?' There wasn't a trace of anger in his voice but a pleading for her to understand.

'What do you mean, Jack?' There was hurt, bewilderment in Fanny's voice. She took out half a loaf of bread that she'd been saving for him, an apple and two half-sucked sherbet lemons and handed them to him. She'd also found a sliver of soap which her mother often threw away when it had diminished to that size. He took them off her and they disappeared into his pocket immediately.

'We get our water from the pump outside,' Jack said, as his foot idly traced a circle round some buttercups. `We don't have hot water from a tap. We heat it on the range and tip it into the tin bath we drag in front of it once a month. We all take it in turns, my father first, then going down in ages until we're all done. The water gets blacker and blacker. When it's my turn, it's thick black like swill. Doesn't make much difference at that point,' Jack shrugged, 'unless you come here – then it does!' Jack paused. `Some use the river to bathe in but it smells foul. I keep away from that!' Fanny wanted to ask so many questions like 'What was a range?' and 'What did the water pump look like?' and 'How did they flush the toilet?' but all the thoughts were tumbling in her head and the only one that came out was, 'How *did* you get here, Jack?'

A frown flitted across Jack's face. 'I dunno,' he muttered. `There I was lying in the pig meadow, looking at the sky and wondering if things would be different in a hundred years or so. The Old Man In The Sky smiled at me and then I found myself lying in your daisy patch!'

'You know The Old Man In The Sky?' Fanny asked incredulously. 'Tis an old story,' Jack mumbled, embarrassed. 'Tain't true. It's just a story.'

'But it came true,' Fanny replied. 'It came true!'

But by then Jack had disappeared again, leaving Fanny with a lot of unanswered questions.

She tried to think what it must be like to have a bath that was full of filthy water. When she had a bath her mother was cross if there was a faint rim of soap scum on the bath when the water had been emptied. To prevent this, Fanny had peach bubble bath in the water and this stopped the scum from forming. This made her mother happier, too.

When she'd had chance, Fanny had asked her mother how the Victorians had flushed the toilet when they didn't have any water inside. Her mother had said, 'Stop bothering me, I'm trying to do the ironing, Fanny – you do ask a lot of questions!'

Fanny's mother had turned away, dismissing her, but then she turned round. 'It's like your Granddad's privy outside.

Fanny remembered the green wooden shed at the bottom of her Granddad's garden. It had a rickety door that didn't quite shut so that when you sat on the wooden shelf with the bucket underneath you had to press your foot against the door to keep it shut. The wind blew through the gap especially in the winter. Once in the late winter when it was dark at four o'clock in the afternoon and Fanny was staying with her grandparents, she had to go to the toilet urgently. She did not like scurrying down the path or sitting in the dark in the outside toilet but what was worse was that her fingers and toes became frozen very quickly. She had pulled up her knickers hurriedly, once she had finished, and ran all the way back to the house as quickly as she could. Her breath formed little puffs of white cloud in front of her as she did so. It took a long time for her fingers and toes to thaw out once she was inside even though she had spread her fingers out in front of the hot coals of the open fire. Her grandma had smiled at her. 'When I was little,' she said, 'there were only two outside toilets for the whole of the street and it could be very cold waiting.'

Fanny hadn't really understood what her Grandma meant then but it was becoming clearer now that she had met Jack. She wondered who emptied the bucket for the whole street and where they put the contents. Perhaps she would ask Jack that, later.

Granddad's rickety outside toilet always had a hook with cut- up newspaper on it, instead of the soft toilet roll that she had at home. The print came off onto her skin, smearing it grey like Jack's complexion so that she always had to use her Grandma's Pear's soap to wash her hands once she was back in the house. She didn't want the ink to come off onto her clothes.

Fanny's mother had bought twelve toilet rolls which had been on offer. She had stacked a number in the bathroom and stashed the others in a bag under the boiler. When she had gone into the garden to hang the washing up on the line, Fanny had taken one of the rolls and hidden it in her wardrobe. She would give it to Jack later.

Jack reappeared later that afternoon when Fanny was humming along to the bees who were wandering from daisy to daisy. Daddy had decided not to cut the lawn. It would be a wildflower meadow instead, he had declared.. Fanny had already transferred the toilet roll to the back of the greenhouse under a plant pot. She was very excited that Jack could have proper soft toilet roll instead of hard scratchy newspaper.

'What's this?' he exclaimed when she had given it to him, her eyes shining at the thought of how happy he would be.

'Why, it's toilet paper,' a confused Fanny replied, 'instead of newspaper.'

'Newspaper?' Jack looked puzzled, at a loss for words.

Fanny didn't really want to talk about such a delicate subject but she had been very brave taking the soft, pink quilted paper and managing to get it out to Jack without her mother finding out. Fanny jutted her chin out. 'Well, what do you wipe yourself with after you've been to the privy?' There was a determined question in her voice.

Jack fingered the soft paper, pushing it slightly with one finger as though he couldn't quite believe what he was seeing. 'You use this?' he said disbelievingly. 'We use sticks, stones, leaves……' Jack paused for a few seconds before a smile transformed his thin features. 'Keep away from the holly and nettles though – they don't half make you jump.'

Fanny considered this. Once, when she had been on a long car journey and there hadn't been any toilets for miles around, everyone had clambered out of the car to find a tree. She had used a handful of grass to wipe herself with but it wasn't absorbent and really didn't compare with the toilet roll at home. Ever since then, Fanny had always hidden a leaf of toilet paper up her sleeve before any long journey was undertaken. It was very hard imagining what Jack's life was like. Fanny resolved that whenever her mother took advantage of special offers, Jack would benefit. For now though, the rhubarb was pink and tall and crying to be picked. Fanny took a few stems, one of her daddy's onions and a small greyhound cabbage which grew in a separate patch. Jack took them gratefully, his thin, grave countenance breaking into a rare smile as he did so. Fanny remembered that she had some brown and white stripy humbugs in her pocket which her Grandad had given her. She didn't like them much and they had become sticky and stuck to the paper bag. She didn't like the feel of the syrup nor pulling the paper off the sweet, so she withdrew them from her pocket and offered the bag to Jack. He looked inside the bag and delicately pulled a sweet out before popping it in his mouth. He rolled it around his tongue, feeling the sweet coolness drowning his senses. He closed his eyes contentedly until all the sweet had dissolved, then he opened his eyes and simply said, 'Thank you!'

With that, he disappeared, but Fanny remembered thinking that it was the first time that she had heard Jack say 'thank you', as though she had done some glorious thing. It made her feel good.

When Fanny visited her grandma next, she asked her about what happened to the contents of the privy bucket. Grandma was pounding flour and water and yeast in a bowl at the time, before leaving it to prove, but she stopped to answer Fanny's question. 'Why, child,' Fanny's Grandma exclaimed, 'then the nightman would take the buckets and empty them into a cesspit, or sometimes the waste would empty straight into a cesspit instead of a bucket.' There might be three or four buckets or chamber pots to empty in one privy. The privies were wooden sheds that had boards with holes in them to sit on. They weren't private and people from many different families in the same street might use them.'

'What's a cesspit? Fanny asked, twiddling her hair around her finger.

'A cesspit, Fanny's Grandma replied, 'was a specially dug hole and it could be very deep and take many years to fill if they were big enough, but a lot of them weren't built very well, so the contents leaked out into the soil or just flowed out onto the streets.'

Fanny initially thought her Grandma was joking, but Grandma wouldn't joke about things like that. Fanny couldn't imagine what that must have been like. It was bad enough trying to dodge all the dog poo that was lying all over the pavements.

'It would stink, Grandma?' This was a question rather than a statement.

'It certainly did, Fanny,' her Grandma replied softly, 'it certainly did, but away from the towns and cities, families would have a privy and cesspool at the bottom of their garden. That was a little more private and the waste was used as manure on their gardens.

In London, though, the River Thames was an open sewer, and most of the waste got dumped into the river. People used to bathe in that river because there weren't any taps in the houses to provide clean water to wash with. If people wanted water they had to stand at a stop cock which was turned on in the street - but only for a few hours a week. There would often be long queues of people waiting for water. The water came from the Thames, where all the sewage went so, there was a lot of disease. Many children died before they reached the age of five.' In 1832, there was a cholera epidemic which killed over ten thousand Londoners by the time it had finished in 1854.

Cholera is an awful disease. People didn't know about germs then so when people became ill they thought it was due to miasma or bad smell, since the air smelt so bad. Even Florence Nightingale, who was a very famous nurse, thought this sickness was due to miasma. So people kept bathing in the River Thames and taking the water from the stopcocks which came from the River Thames, not realising that it could kill them.

A man called Dr John Snow began to think that the cause of cholera was not miasma. He thought that cholera was carried in the water. He had lots of evidence which he gave to the people in authority who were responsible for the health of the people in Soho, but no one would believe him and he died during the time called 'The Great Stink'.'

'The Great Stink!' Fanny echoed, hanging onto Grandma's every word.

'Yes, `The Great Stink`, Grandma confirmed. 'The River Thames was so polluted - so thick and black - that it forced the politicians to do something about it. They decided to ask a man called Joseph Bazalgette to design a sewage system which would take the waste far away from where people were living to a different part of the river. Bazalgette's sewage pipes took all the waste to the Thames estuary, which is lower down the river and which is connected to the sea. It wasn't anywhere near where people lived, so that made disease less likely and, of course, it eventually stopped 'The Great Stink'.'

'If London was so bad to live in,' Fanny began, 'why did people live there?'

Fanny's grandma stopped what she was doing. She looked as though she was thinking deeply. Her eyes appeared to be distant, 'There was a lot of poverty in the countryside and work was very hard to come by. It might be that you were only needed for a few weeks to work as a labourer on a farm at harvest time and then the work dried up. Living in the country might be healthier but there wasn't much money, so people migrated to the large towns in search of work and prosperity. There were always epidemics of disease, such as typhus carried by lice, and cholera and typhoid carried by polluted water. If only they'd known to boil their drinking water........... My own grandfather, Firth died from typhus when he was 35, leaving three small children and an unborn child.'

Fanny listened intently. She had never really thought about her grandma having grandparents, although she knew that she must have had. She just knew that her daddy's family had belonged to generations of farmers and when Fanny had asked her mother what her family had which belonged to them, her mother had remained tight -lipped. Later in the evening, Fanny had overheard her daddy saying to her mother, 'Really darling, there is no shame in being the great granddaughter of an honest labourer, even if the family did end up in the workhouse. Things are very different now.'

Chapter Four

Jack did not appear for many days. Fanny had stashed away a great deal of food as well as some cast-off clothes for Jack which her brother did not require any more, since he had outgrown them. She had also found some aspirin in a dusty bottle at the back of the medicine cabinet which she was forbidden to go into. If she had been caught, it would have meant a week of having to go to bed early and having to lie in bed when daylight still tantalisingly illuminated the room as a reminder of missed adventures and opportunities. She had also found a bottle of malt — a concoction which her mother poured down her throat at every opportunity during the winter. The thick musty blackness made Fanny gag and it never did appear to reduce the sore throats that she kept getting through the winter months. The malt also went into the bag of goodies which Fanny had saved for Jack, so Fanny was excited about collecting these things yet frustrated when he failed to appear.

When Jack finally appeared in the middle of the daisy patch some Sundays later - following Fanny's eighth birthday - he looked much older and thinner than Fanny remembered him. He still sat back in his languid fashion, propped up and with his arms behind him and his legs crossed in front of him. However, the ends of his tattered breeches now reached much further up his painfully thin limbs, and some of his cheekiness had drained out of him. He seemed hollow, uncertain.

'Maria died. And Arthur and Robert.' Jack paused and then carried on softly as though speaking to himself, 'and the twins Martin and Albert and………. my dad.'

Fanny didn't know what to say. She stuck her thumb in her mouth and tried to separate out all the things in her head she'd heard grown-ups utter when someone had died, so that she could choose which one to say. Instead, none seemed appropriate, so she remained quiet. Jack had by this time picked up Fanny's art pad, along with the HB pencil and crayons, and begun to draw idly on the paper. At first, with concentration etched into his face, his fingers worked slowly and methodically. But then they began to work faster, and as he gathered pace, he added minute detail. The fascinated Fanny watched as, slowly, the pinched faces of Jack's siblings slowly came to life. There was two year old Maria with dimples and golden curls, and a slightly older Robert, not unlike her with his fair hair and dimples. Arthur looked older than Jack, but, unlike Maria and Robert, his colouring was darker, his air graver, his cheeks hollower. The twins Martin and Albert were less than a year old. Jack had drawn them asleep as though it was kinder that they did not have to look out on the world which did not care if they lived or died. Finally, Jack added his father. Jack's father looked old – older than Fanny's Grandad - although Jack said he was only thirty five. The harshness of life had etched itself into his face, the skin stretched taut over the sunken, sallow cheeks.

Fanny could feel the tears trickling down her cheeks. She had tried to hold them back but a deep ache had started in her chest before rising and spilling out of her. She tried to stifle her sobs, for Jack was not sentimental. His world did not have time for sympathy. Fanny thought she heard Jack mutter 'Fewer mouths to feed,' as though repeating to himself what he'd heard many times before. Fanny thought she had misheard him because it seemed a peculiar thing to say.

Under the drawing, Jack had written 1853. It was the only thing that Jack knew how to write and his handwriting was coarse, broken and childlike. Fanny added the names of each family member under each of the pictures, using her best joined-up writing.

'What did they die of?' she asked, looking at Jack from under the safety of her bangs.

'Cholera.' He replied abruptly, throwing the pencil into the daisy patch.' 'It's just me, Thomas, William and me Ma now.'

Fanny remembered her grandma saying that the cholera epidemics lasted from 1832 until 1854 in London. Cholera was caused by contaminated water and gave the sufferers such bad diarrhoea that they were likely to die from dehydration. There was no point in drinking water to try and cure it. The water in the stop taps came from the filthy sewage filled River Thames. It would just continue to cause disease whenever it was drunk.

'You should have boiled the water,' Fanny murmured, more to herself than for Jack's benefit.

'Huh?' There was a questioning in Jack's voice.

Fanny repeated what she had said, adding that her grandma had once told her about cholera and that it was caused by a germ which could be killed if the water was boiled for three minutes.

Jack listened intently but didn't reply, so Fanny took the bag which contained all the goodies that she had saved for him and passed it over. A foil-wrapped piece of her birthday cake fell out. Jack picked it up and carefully unfolded the foil. 'What is it?' he asked, sniffing the cake, poking his finger into the moist icing and slipping his iced finger into his mouth.

'It was my birthday cake,' Fanny explained. 'I was eight some two weeks ago. How old are you Jack?'

'I dunno……… maybe nine or ten …..'

'You don't know how old you are?' Fanny asked incredulously.

'What difference does it make?' Jack responded wearily as he continued to eat morsels of cake in a delicate and restrained way which belied the ravenous hunger he felt.

Fanny thought of how excited she became when her birthdays approached. She always made a list of presents to give to her relatives and, no matter how long the list was, she nearly always received all the presents that she wanted. Her mother would allow two of her friends around for a birthday tea that would include sausage rolls, jelly and a birthday cake with candles. Birthdays were a special occasion which Fanny looked forward to a great deal, and she couldn't imagine not knowing when her birthday was.

Jack had already finished his cake. He wiped his hand across his mouth and remarked on how good it tasted before opening the bag that Fanny had filled with all sorts of things for his family. Fanny didn't know how Jack would react to being given her brother's clothes. What Jack wore and what her brother wore were entirely different. Jack seemed to sense her thoughts. 'My ma's a seamstress,' he said.

'A seamstress?' Asked Fanny.

'Yes, she sews clothes for the rich, fifteen hours a day. Her fingers are stiff and sore all the time.' Jack stopped and then suddenly began to sing in a flat kind of voice.

With fingers weary and worn

With eyelids heavy and red,
A woman sat, in unwomanly rags,
Plying her needle and thread
Stitch, stitch, stitch,
In poverty, hunger and dirt
And still with a voice of dolorous pitch
She sang the 'Song of the Shirt.'

Work! Work! Work
While the cock is crowing aloof!
And work, work , work
Till the stars shine through the roof!
It's Oh! To be a slave
Along with the barbarous Turk,
Where woman has never a soul to save,
If this is Christian work.

Work, work, work,
Till the brain begins to swim,
Work, work, work
Till the eyes are heavy and dim!

Seam and gusset, and band,
Band and gusset and seam,
Till over the buttons I fall asleep,
And sew them on in a dream!
'Oh, Men with Sisters dear!
Oh men, with Mothers and Wives
It is not linen you're wearing out,
But human creatures lives!
Stitch, stitch, stitch,
In poverty, hunger and dirt,
Sewing at once, with a double thread,
A shroud as well as a shirt

'But why do I talk of Death?
That phantom of grisly bone,
I hardly fear it's terrible shape,
It seems so like my own
Because of the fasts I keep
Oh God! That bread should be so dear
And flesh and blood so cheap!

Work, work, work!
My labour never flags
And what are its wage? A bed of straw
A crust of bread and rags.
That shattered roof, this naked floor
A table and a broken chair
And a wall so blank, my shadow I thank
For sometimes falling there!

Work, work work!
From weary chime to chime
Work, work work
As prisoners work for crime!
Band and gusset, and seam,
Seam and gusset and band
Till the heart is sick and the brain benumbed,
As well as the weary hand

'Tis a poem called 'Song of the Shirt,' by Thomas Hood,' Jack muttered, looking embarrassed at his learning. He's a Victorian poet. 'I know all the verses.' And he continued,

Work, work, work

In the dull December light,

When the weather is warm and bright

While underneath the eaves

The brooding swallows cling

As if to show me their sunny backs

And twit me with the spring.

Oh! But to breathe the breath

Of the cowslip and primrose sweet

With the sky above my head,

And the earth beneath my feet,

For only one short hour

To feel as I used to feel

Before I knew the woes of want

And the walk that costs a meal

Fanny's heart had grown sadder and heavier as Jack had recited the poem. It wasn't a happy poem in the way that her grandma was happy sewing her grandad's patches on his elbows or taking up the hems on his trousers or sewing on the big brown buttons on his waistcoats. It was a joyless and despairing. Sadness had oozed its way into Fanny in a way she had not experienced before. She clapped her hands over her ears, 'Stop, Jack,' she cried, 'It is so sad. Please stop!'

Jack did stop, his small body quivering with emotion, but whether it was anger or sadness or something else, Fanny did not know. She did not want Jack to speak while she tried to process the thought about never being able to breathe in the delicate perfume of the cowslip and the primrose. She loved the freshness of newly mown grass and the fragrance of the apricot roses which wafted on the breeze, mingling with the unmistakeable sharpness of the lemon scented pelargoniums. Fanny hated being inside and the thought of having to stitch all day until the fingers were red raw and bleeding was incomprehensible. She felt hot and overwhelmed, as though the world was going to collapse in on her. At times like this, Fanny would normally retreat to her room and pull the heavy scratchy blankets around her until she felt safe and cocooned, but Jack was still standing there, a slight figure, unsure now of what to do. He hadn't disappeared, it wasn't his time yet. Fanny spread her hands gently over the daisies. Some buttercups had sprung up amongst them, stretching their golden faces upwards towards the slowly fading late afternoon sun. A shadow trailed itself across her legs and she looked up. A cloud had drifted silently across the face of the sun. The dragon transitioned momentarily into the Old Man of the Sky. He beamed at her from his lofty height, and as he did so, Fanny had a startling thought which was scary and frightening at the same time. She turned to face Jack before taking a deep breath.

'I would like to come to Victorian London with you, Jack. Do you think that is possible?'

Fanny thought that Jack was going to reply, but he vanished, along with the bag that she had filled for him before he could reply. A cheeky robin hopped over, tipping his head over so that his beady black eyes could take in the crumbs which were left on the daisy patch after Jack had eaten the birthday cake. It was really the only sign that Jack had been, although somewhere floating on the air, the words of the 'Song of the Shirt' could be heard....

'Oh! But for one short hour!

A respite however brief!

No blessed leisure for Love or Hope

But only time for Grief!

A little weeping would ease my heart,

But in their briny bed

Fanny and Victorian Jack

My tears must stop, for every drop

Hinders needle and thread

Chapter Five

Fanny did not get much chance to visit the daisy patch after that for a number of weeks. The summer's rain, which had been forecast to last for only a couple of days, continued to fall, dampening not only the earth but the spirits of the people around Fanny. Only Daddy appeared grateful for the rain, since this meant that he didn't have to go out and water the plants every day. Besides which, he had plenty of other things to do. Fanny took this opportunity to ask Daddy about Victorian England.

'What sort of houses did people live in, in Victorian England?' Fanny asked her daddy when he was trying to fix a plug.

He looked up. 'Are you doing a project at school on the Victorians? You seem to be very interested in that era.' He didn't wait for an answer but continued, 'Well, the early years of Queen Victoria's reign were very exciting, because it was a time when new machines were being invented and huge factories were being built to house them. The machines, which were powered by steam, meant that more goods could be made more quickly. However, this also meant that more coal was needed to smelt the iron and steel needed to make these machines; and, of course, coal was needed to provide fuel for steam engines. All this began in the late 1700's and was given a special name. It was called the Industrial Revolution.'

'What does smelting mean?' asked Fanny, who was trying to take everything in.

Fanny's daddy paused, as though trying to recollect something that he hadn't thought about for a long time. 'When the iron is taken out of the ground,' he continued, 'it is usually in the form of iron ore which is iron all mixed up with stony bits of the earth and chemicals. It is also mixed with loose earth called gangue. The gangue can easily be washed out, but the hard iron and stone which are all mixed up together have to be smelted. This means heating the ore up until it becomes softer – like sponge - and the chemicals and the stony bits break down, leaving behind just the iron.'

Fanny thought that this all sounded like a lot of hard work just to get some iron out of the earth. Besides which, she was more interested in the people who were living in the Industrial Revolution.   Fortunately, her daddy started talking about the people again.

'There wasn't a great deal of work in the countryside, so people started moving to the cities to find jobs in the new factories and the factory owners built rows of back-to-back tiny houses for their workers to live in. The industrial towns, like London, were very unhealthy. The factory chimneys belched out thick black smoke, which damaged people's lungs and so they didn't live very long. Disease spread quickly because of the poor sanitation.   The workers weren't paid very much and bread was very expensive because of the Corn Laws.

'What were the Corn Laws,' Fanny asked, trying to picture what her daddy was talking, about even though it was quite horrible to contemplate.

'Well, the Government wanted people to buy food that was grown in their own country so they placed a tax on any food or grain that was imported from other countries, often making it very expensive for the Victorian Poor to buy. Bread was their staple diet and they might have some dripping on it and a few mouldy vegetables to go with it. Sometimes, this might be just potato peelings. Once a week, on a Sunday, they might have meat.

Some of the bakers might cheat their customers by adding Plaster of Paris — a plaster-mould powder made from gypsum - to the flour. They might also add alum which was a chemical that made the bread look whiter. Shopkeepers might dilute the milk with water to make it go further. Parliament had to pass laws to punish those people who cheated their customers.

The areas in the cities which were overcrowded and of poor quality were called slums. The richer people did not approve of them and many of the slums were demolished when roads were cut through them. This didn't really help because the families had to go somewhere and so would move in with other families. That might mean that four or five adults would crowd into one bed and the children might lie at the foot of the bed or on the floor.

There often wasn't anywhere to cook in those dreadful places, so families had to buy their food from street vendors. The street vendors sold food like hot potatoes, pies, hot soup, sheep's trotters or roasted chestnuts.'

Fanny pulled a face at the mention of sheep's trotters. Her mother often gave her lamb stew, and that had a lot of gristle in it. She thought that sheep's trotters probably also had a lot of gristle attached to them. Fanny didn't like a lot of food that her mother served up, including toast, scrambled egg, gristle, fish and oranges. Her mother called her a 'fussy child' who 'would be the death of her', but Fanny was convinced that she would not have liked any of the food that the poor Victorians ate. No, not at all. In fact, Victorian life for children just didn't sound much fun at all. It seemed that even her pet hamster Tilly had better food to eat than the children of the Victorian poor.

Fanny's daddy ruffled her hair in his usual way. 'Things are a bit different now, aren't they? Of course, I'll swear that your mother gives us sheep's trotters now and again, judging by the amount of gristle that we have in that stew of hers!' He started rifling in his tool box, which signalled to Fanny that he must be allowed to get on with all his odd jobs.

Fanny was glad though, that it wasn't only her that didn't like the gristle. She had once tried to give some to Tilly, too. Tilly had just sniffed at it, turned away and clambered onto her wheel, refusing to go into the corner of the cage where Fanny had placed the gristle, until Fanny had picked it out. She had then thrown the gristle away onto the waste ground at the very top of the garden, and a beady-eyed magpie danced momentarily on the fence top before swooping down and grasping it in his claws. Fanny had seen magpies in action before on roadkill, where the piebald birds would tear the last of the flesh from an unfortunate rabbit that had been dazzled by the headlights of an oncoming car.

'They're thieves!' her grandma had once said. 'Those magpies will take anything they can get hold off. They kill the juvenile blackbirds if they can get hold of them in the spring. The parents always kick them out of the nest a fortnight before they can fly and they just have to hide in the undergrowth away from marauders like the magpies!'

Fanny was disappointed to find that the rain was still spattering against the windows, meaning that the daisy patch was out of reach. She had tried earlier to go outside, pulling on her pink wellingtons and cagoule quite nonchalantly as though it was the most normal thing in the world to want to play out in the pouring rain.

'Just what do you think you are doing?' her mother had asked when she caught Fanny zipping up her cagoule. 'It's too wet to play outside. Take those things off at once and come and help me make the beds!' Fanny's mother's mouth had set hard, which meant that Fanny didn't have an option. It was either helping with the beds or an early night for her.

Fanny didn't mind pulling the sheets off. She would be especially glad to take the yellow, brushed-nylon sheet off her bed because the feel of the material against her skin was uncomfortable and strange, in the same way as gristle and fish bones. There was only one brushed-nylon sheet, which Fanny's mother had been delighted to find in a sale. This meant that the cool candy-stripe cotton sheet would almost certainly find its way onto her bed. This material didn't make her feel hot and itchy, unlike the brushed-nylon. She dropped the yellow sheet onto the floor, kicking it under the bed. She might not like it, she thought, it but Jack might. She wondered if she should let her mother wash it first, but then she thought of Jack in his filthy patched breeches and considered that washing it probably wouldn't make much difference anyway. Anyway, it would probably be the cleanest thing that he had!

Right at the bottom of the pile of sheets in the cupboard were a couple of old towels. They were obviously in the wrong pile. Fanny couldn't ever remember them hanging over the side of the bath so that probably meant that her mother had forgotten about them too. She waited until her mother had slipped downstairs before retrieving the towels and adding them to the bundle for Jack. She slid the bundle right to the back of the bed. It would be safe there. Her mother only pulled the beds out once a month to clean under them. Fanny once mentioned this when Mrs Beaumont, the neighbour, had been chatting over the fence to her mother. Fanny had been sent inside sharply and given a good talking to. Apparently, even though the beds were only pulled out and vacuumed less often than once a month, on the occasions that the neighbours – or indeed anyone else - were listening, Fanny had to remain silent, or failing that, say that the beds were pulled out and cleaned under, every week.

Fanny pressed her nose to the window. The raindrops, frustratingly, still made their way down the pane in tiny rivulets before joining and pooling on the sill. The sky was soft and grey, as though apologising for intruding and ruining Fanny's day.

Fanny followed one tiny rivulet down with her finger. 'Where are you Jack?' she whispered softly, 'where are you?'

Fanny could hear the clock ticking in the silence and the faint pitter-patting of the raindrops on the window. A door creaked, a stair tread groaned. There was another faint sound, but Fanny had to strain to make out the distant but rhythmic

'With fingers weary and worn,

With eyelids heavy and red,

A woman sat in unwomanly rags,

Plying her needle and thread

Stitch! Stitch! Stitch!

In poverty, hunger and dirt

And still with a voice of dolorous pitch

Would that its tone could reach the Rich!

She sang this 'Song of the Shirt!'

Chapter Six

The stench had hit Fanny's throat, causing her to gag, even before she opened her eyes. When she did so, Jack was standing by her in a damp tiny room, not much bigger than Fanny's bedroom at home. 'You'll get used to it.' Jack said kindly. He seemed a taller, more confident person now than Fanny had seen before, but then, he was in his own time! He took off his cloth cap and swept it across his body with a flourish, so that clouds of thick, choking dust rose before settling once again. 'Welcome to Victorian England ..... Jack Bones at your service, your ladyship.'

The thick, stinky smell had begun to entwine itself around Fanny like an invisible python. It seemed as if every time that she took a breath it was becoming more and more a part of her. She tried to breathe less but that didn't work: just a few shallow breaths meant that she had to take a deeper one later, and all the while she wanted to retch this bad air – this miasma - out of her. Fanny did not know how Jack could live with it.

The room was all wrong, too, containing a bed and a table and two chairs all in the same space. Old, frayed rugs hung limply on the walls. They were even older and more ragged than the ones grandma threw out for granddad to use in his garage. Damp glistened on the bare patches even though the dying embers of the fire suggested that the fire had been burning for a while. Pots and pans hung silently from hooks in the ceiling, washing hung loosely off a line stretching across the back of the room.

For a moment, Fanny forgot the thick choking stench of sewage and smoke. There was too much to take in, so she had to just deal with one thing at a time. When things had been too overwhelming at home, she had simply taken herself off to bed and wrapped the quilt around her thickly until it blocked out all sight and sound. Once she was safely enveloped in her comforter, she was able to examine in detail the events and information which had been bothering her, until she felt able to emerge from her cocoon. There had been times when Fanny had not been able to reach the safety of her bedroom. All the sights and sounds and smells had kept exploding in her head until she couldn't think straight. What was worse was that people had kept talking to her, adding to her confusion until she had clapped her hands over her ears and shut her eyes to drown out all the commotion. Fanny's mother had given her a hard slap for 'being so rude and showing me up in front of the neighbours'. But Fanny was so distressed at this point that she hardly felt the slap, although it left a deep red handprint on her leg where her mother's hand had made contact.

Fanny took a deep breath –though this was probably the wrong thing to do given the stench that invaded her being every time she breathed - but Jack was looking at her with concern. There wasn't a bed with a thick soft quilt on it to wrap around her nor could she sit down, clap her hands over her ears and scream to try and drown out everything that was threatening to overwhelm her.

'What do we do now?' Fanny asked in a quiet voice, so that she did not have to deeply inhale the stench. 'It is so dark in here!' she uttered. She couldn't see where the light switches were.

Jack thrust his hands into his pockets. 'We need to save the candles so me Ma can sew later,' he said, pointing to a neat pile of cloth on the chair and smiling as he did so. Some of it looked remarkably like Fanny's brother's old clothing, but it had somehow been cut and shaped differently, and was waiting to be sewn. Jack bowed before stepping towards the door, which wasn't much higher than Fanny. 'Let me show you London, your ladyship!' Jack continued, stretching out his hand to beckoning Fanny to go first.

Fanny hesitated. This was a little too much to expect. She would look out of place in her fancy shoes with their tiny bows, and the party dress that her mother had made for her. The cotton dress, printed with butterflies, had sent Fanny into raptures when she first saw it. She has subsequently worn it at every opportunity, tracing her finger over each printed butterfly.

Jack pushed her gently, as though being able to read her thoughts. 'It's Ok!' he muttered. 'Things will change when they are meant to change.'

Fanny didn't understand what Jack meant but as soon as she hesitantly stepped straight outside into the narrow cobbled street, her dress had changed into a coarse brown cloth, patched with many squares of mismatched material. The cotton smock did not look much better and the bonnet which now rested on her head was stained and too small.

'Better keep it on,' Jack advised. 'It stops you from getting lice off other people.'

Fanny thought Jack was joking, but one look at his face and she could see that he wasn't.

'Where's my shoes?' Fanny asked. 'I can't go out without shoes!'

'You'll fit in now,' Jack replied briefly, as though that answered her question.

The street which Fanny had stepped into was very narrow. Tall, blackened walls excluded the light, casting eerie shadows in the afternoon's light. Laundry hung from windows flapping malevolently as a gust of wind forced its way through the narrow aperture at the end of the back lane. A stop tap drip dripped onto the cobbles, smoothing out a hollowed area in the rounded dome of one of the cobbles. A dog had obligingly filled it and moved on.

`Ugh! Dog poo!' Fanny shuddered violently. She had bare feet, and everywhere she looked there appeared to be something that she had to avoid. If it wasn't dog waste, it was human waste. What if she stepped into it? She would not be able to bear that, and if she couldn't wrap herself up into her duvet then she would end up having a 'proper strop' as her mother called it. She lifted up her skirts delicately and trod carefully.

There were mazes of these imposing back-to-back terraced houses. As soon as Fanny had picked her way through one row, her path would open out into an identical row. She knew that if it hadn't been for Jack, she would have become lost and disorientated very quickly. Sometimes a small raggedy child would be sitting against the wall, the greying complexion, matted hair and too-thin features making Fanny's kind heart sadden. The children did not appear to have the energy to move, so only their pleading and desperate eyes followed Fanny. She went to feel in her pocket for a sucked humbug before realising that her Victorian clothing did not carry such luxuries in their pocket. Somehow, but somehow, she would find a way to help.

The rows of houses began to open out. Men in tattered shirts with bow ties, coats down to their knees and patched trousers, walked hunched over as though the effort of living was too much for them. They looked grey and old as though the filth of the city had oozed into their skin and hair forever.

Vendors began to appear, wearing tattered clothing, tattered bonnets and tattered shoes. 'Come and get yer whelks, luvvie,' one woman cried, exposing a row of blackened teeth which reminded Fanny of the witch in one of her fairy-tale books.

'A pint o' milk for a penny dear?'

'Hot potatoes! Hot potatoes! Come and get yer hot potatoes.'

'Bread, just thruppence a loaf!'

If, at that moment, Fanny had felt hungry then all hunger disappeared as she looked at the stained clothing and filthy hands of the vendors. Her mother had always taught her the importance of washing her hands well before meals and touching food and that if she did drop some food down her clothes, she had to change them immediately. Otherwise, what would the neighbours say?

A tiny waif of a girl sat on the pavement with a tray of matches balanced precariously on her lap. Whenever someone walked up the street she would grasp a fistful and reach out to the passer-by. 'Buy me matches, Mister,' she would plead.

Fanny was shocked to see that the little girl's teeth were missing or rotting. Her jaw seemed too big for the rest of her frail body and, as Fanny moved nearer she could smell the foulness of the little girl's breath.

' She's got 'phossy jaw'. She's worked in the match factory,' Jack explained. 'She's had to dip the matches into phosphorus …….. rots the teeth …. but if yer breathes it in too often, yer dies. It's cheaper to pay a child than an adult, but they get sicker quickly…………   'Just one less mouth to feed.'

'Can't the doctors make her better?' Fanny asked, feeling desperately sad for the little girl.

'Only way is to take her jaw out,' Jack answered briefly. `Better to die.'

Fanny remembered a story she had read once about a little matchstick girl. She had thought it was just a fairy-tale and not something that was based on real life.

Jack started singing softly under his breath

'The factory owners are made rich and fat

Off the back of the workers

They'll flog us until we're fit to drop

Cos they don't want no shirkers.'

'There's rag gatherers, bone collectors and pure collectors on these streets if you want to make an honest living,' Jack laughed, as though the thought had amused him, `but you have to be quick, the rags and bones get swooped on quickly enough.'

'What's a pure collector?' Fanny asked innocently. This at least sounded a better job than a rag or bone collector.

Pure was good. The wrapping on her soap at home advertised 'pure soap' as though it was something very special.

'Dog turd!' replied Jack briefly, 'Eight pennies a bucket, maybe ten if it's yer lucky day. Pigeon dung, too. Tanners use it! In a good week you could collect up to eight buckets. Mind, you'd have to take it home until the bucket was full. There's a lot of light fingers around here!'

'Light fingers .... tanners...............?' Fanny stammered uncomprehendingly.

'Thieves have light fingers,' Jack explained, 'and tanners make leather from animal hides. They soak the blood stained animal hides in lime pits in which is a mixture of dog turds and water to help rot them down and make them softer.'

'That's gross!' Fanny shuddered violently. 'That is the worst thing that I have ever heard of!' One thing was for sure: she was never going to wear her leather shoes again!

Something caught Jack's eye. It was a fat brown cigar butt which had been casually thrown away. He stooped down, rolling it around in his fingers before slipping it into his pocket. `I reckon I can make summat out of this,' he muttered, 'Maybe worth a penny or two.'

A thought crossed Fanny's mind. 'Will I get to meet William and Thomas, do you think. I would like to meet them.'

'Anything's possible, I suppose,' replied Jack, `but I don't know how long you're here for and they're both out.. Thomas is out at the factory and William's a gardener's boy. It's long days .... up at five am and home at nine pm for Thomas. William has half a day Saturday off and all day Sunday . They're both exhausted when they get in but it pays the rent and puts food on the table. The household William works at allows him to bring some home-grown vegetables back, maybe an egg or two if the chickens have laid well. It's a better life than Thomas has.'

'What does Thomas do?' Fanny enquired, scratching her head where the coarse bonnet had made her feel very warm and very itchy.

'He cleans the machines from the crack of dawn until late at night. They're still running while he cleans them. He's not allowed to talk or sit down or look out of the window. Work! Work! Work!' Last week George Brook had three of his fingers ripped off in the machine and the week before that Mary Jane got her hair caught in the machinery – tore her scalp right off. Thomas is still having nightmares about that.'

Fanny didn't need to ask if Mary Jane was still alive, for somehow she knew that she wasn't. Children were cheap labour, they couldn't complain and their tiny, thin bodies were ideal for crawling under the machinery to clean it.

'Anyway,' Jack continued, 'a child's life is cheap – there's plenty more in the orphanages and living on the streets to replace the likes of George and Mary Jane. In 1833 a Factory Act was made law. It was made illegal for children under the age of nine to be employed in textile factories. Some factory owners keep to that, some don't. They didn't with George and Mary Jane, that's for sure.'

'How old are Thomas and William?' Fanny asked, trying desperately to scratch one leg with the bare toes of her other foot. Really, this coarse skirt was unbearably itchy and the flies which had been following her and flying around her head were really beginning to annoy her. She tried to slap one quickly and squash it on her leg but, annoyingly for Fanny, it flew off.

'Dunno!' Jack muttered, 'Mebbe seven or eight. Who knows?'

Jack paused, shaking his head slightly so that flakes of soot flew off onto Fanny's smock. `If the cholera, typhoid and work don't kill you, the summer diarrhoea will.'

'Summer diarrhoea?' Fanny echoed questioningly.

'Look around, Fanny,' Jack implored her.

Fanny took her eyes of the cobbles, hoping she would not tread on any dog waste. The flies which had been bothering her were swarming on the streets, feeding off horse manure and human waste. Fanny could hear them buzzing. It sounded hostile and threatening, unlike the friendly hum of a honey bee as it danced from flower to flower on a warm summer's day. Fanny shivered. She hoped Jack would return her to his slum dwelling soon, away from the filth and the noise of Victorian London. Jack had reached the end of the street where the vendors plied their trade. A turn of the corner revealed huge factories belching out thick black smoke into the air. No wonder that the air smelt different to the clean pure air that Fanny breathed in at home. It smelt polluted, and there was no doubting that. Fanny could see now why the buildings were blackened with soot and the fresh washing that hung out of the windows of the slums was a dirty grey colour. There was no chance of the washing turning out spotless even if the water it had been washed in was clean. Fanny understood now why people everywhere were coughing, wheezing and spitting into the street. She pulled her smock over her nose as she had seen her mother do with her apron when someone near her had sneezed.

'Death stalks this city,' Jack said darkly. 'What life have we here but about twenty five years, yet in the countryside twice as much or more.'

Jack had started retracing his steps back through the filth of the cobbled streets which caused all sorts of diseases, the flapping washing and the smutty, blackened buildings. His nimble feet and watchful eyes were accustomed to avoiding the very worst of the streets of the London slums and, like a shadow, he appeared to move and be noticed by no-one. It seemed safer that way.

Clara Bones was sitting in the chair next to the fire when Jack and Fanny finally appeared back at the slum dwelling. Clara Bones was a tiny birdlike woman with braided hair coiled tightly on her head. She wore a brown woollen skirt, cotton blouse and a cotton smock, not unlike Fanny's, but it was not this that Fanny really noticed first. For Clara's arms were no thicker than her own, and her fingers - just skin and bone – were red and raw from sewing. Deep shadows hollowed her eyes above yellow, pinched cheeks. Death, it appeared, was also stalking Clara Bones, yet Clara Bones did not appear to be surprised at Fanny's appearance in her dwelling. She bit off a length of cotton and held the needle to the light to thread it before pointing to the pile of material which had once been Fanny's brother's cast offs and murmuring 'Thank you!'

Fanny realised that she was once again wearing her proper clothes and that a couple of humbugs were still lying in her pocket. She could feel their stickiness as her fingers reached into the cool cotton pocket before she pulled the humbugs out and proffered them firstly to Jack's Ma and then to Jack himself. Fanny watched while the pair of them slowly sucked their sweets with a look of pure joy on their faces. It really was worth giving up her humbugs for.

'Fanny! Fanny! Fanny!' The voice was becoming more urgent and more insistent now. Jack and his mother had disappeared and only blackness remained. She felt a tugging and her mother's voice angrily saying, 'Oh, there you are, curled up in your quilt again, expecting me to always be chasing after you. What have you been doing, Fanny? You smell like a sewer. Don't tell me I'll have to wash all your bedding. Go and get washed now. It's scrambled eggs for tea!'

Chapter Seven

It was the beginning of the long summer holidays. Fanny was glad that she didn't have to go to school, but her mother had 'had enough of her' and allowed her to go and stay with her grandparents so that she could have a rest. For Fanny, this really wasn't a punishment at all since Grandma never made scrambled eggs on toast and did not mind if Fanny didn't eat her crusts up. Grandma simply put them out on the window ledge for the cheeky robin. Grandma did not have a quilt to roll up in at her house. On Fanny's bed were blankets of knitted squares in all shades of colours, all neatly edged with yellow crochet. They did not 'hug' Fanny in the same way that the quilt could, but that did not matter since Fanny had never had a meltdown at her grandparents.

Her mother said that Grandad was a 'bad influence', since he had once let Fanny have a puff on his pipe. Fanny had coughed and spluttered as her lips had closed around the pipe before pulling it away sharply. 'I am never, never going to smoke ever, it's disgusting!' she announced to Grandad firmly. Grandad simply smiled with a knowing look on his face.

Instead of scrambled eggs on toast, Grandma made Cornish pasties with thick gravy, followed by apple pie and thick Bird's custard. Grandma never made lamb. She cooked brisket of beef in the 'long slow oven' and baked huge towering clouds of Yorkshire pudding in the 'hot oven.' This was a delightful meal but one which Grandma explained was only served on a Sunday in the homes of the Victorian poor.'

'Only meat on a Sunday?' an astonished Fanny had asked. 'What did they eat on other days?'

Her Grandma nodded. 'Just meat on a Sunday, and then children had to sit down and eat every scrap without speaking. They could only speak if they were spoken to. On other days it might be bread and dripping or gruel or maybe a few old and often rotten vegetables.''

How many times had Fanny heard her mother say, 'Don't speak until you are spoken to!' Maybe that was to stop you complaining if you were given a dish of rotting vegetables. No wonder the Victorian poor had looked so ill.

'What happened if people became ill?' Fanny asked, knowing that if she ate rotten vegetables she would have a very upset tummy.

'There wasn't a lot of good medicine around', Grandma answered, sifting flour into a bowl. `Sometimes a doctor would attach a leech to someone and draw a little blood. The leech gatherers weren't very well-paid. When they collected the leeches they had to wade through bogs and marshes and allow them to cling onto their legs. Then they would pull off all the leeches that had collected on their legs and throw them into a bucket. It could also make them very ill indeed if the leeches took too much of their blood. Sometimes the wounds where the leeches sucked blood became infected with bacteria, too. The work was seasonal because you can only find leeches in the warmer months. It wasn't a nice job'

Fanny couldn't think of any job in Victorian England which sounded pleasant.

'And, of course,' her Grandma continued, 'they used herbs like plantain.'

Fanny knew what plantain was for; she often helped her Daddy dig it up out of the lawn.

'Plantain was a very common herb and its leaves were sometimes used to make tea that people drank. It was said to help cure common coughs.' Grandma shuddered as though recalling a long distant event and, seeing Fanny's questioning look, added, 'I had it once but it didn't taste too good. Then there was the Everlasting Pill. The Everlasting Pill was invented because the Victorians thought that badness inside you caused a lot of disease. The pill was made of a metal called antimony, which was poisonous, and when you swallowed it, it caused violent vomiting and diarrhoea. The Victorians thought this was a good way of getting rid of all the badness in the body. When the pill disappeared down the privy, they would retrieve it, wash it and put it back on the shelf for the next person to use. Some people made a lot of money out of the misery of others.'

Fanny shivered at the thought of the Everlasting Pill but didn't say anything in case she interrupted Grandma, who had taken a deep breath and was ready to continue her story.

'Sometimes the Victorians would use plasters to draw the badness out of someone's body. The plasters were made out of thin leather on which was pasted a blend of wax and other ingredients such as lead. The people would buy them and put them on whatever part of their body was thought to be producing the illness. Some of the plasters were very large. Of course, they didn't make people better because the cause of their illness wasn't the badness or 'humours' the Victorians believed it was.' Grandma slid her knife through half a pound of creamy yellow butter, chopping it up into smaller dollops before adding it to the sifted flour. Then, taking her fingers, she began to rub the fat into the flour until it resembled breadcrumbs.

'Fetch me a couple of those Bramleys apples, Fanny. There's a good girl.'

Fanny skipped to the top of the scullery stairs where a small shelf was set into the underside of the ceiling. This was where her Grandma kept the vegetables and some of the fruit which had to be prepared before it was eaten.

The shelf was always teeming with vegetables. Grandad and his neighbour were keen vegetable growers and they swapped what they grew for something different that a neighbour had grown, meaning that there was always a good variety of home- grown produce to be had.

Grandma added some cinnamon to the mix and a little sugar. The apples were peeled, cored, chopped and laid in the bottom of a metal dish. Grandma was rifling around in the cupboard under the sink. 'Oh! Here it is!' she exclaimed as she produced a small plastic baking dish, the sort that didn't melt if you put it in the oven. 'Now you can make your own apple crumble, Fanny!'

Fanny scooped generous amounts of apple into the dish and covered it liberally with crumble mix before allowing Grandma to put it into the oven.

While the crumble was baking, Grandma took out a drawer which contained pieces of material, old tablecloths, spools of cotton and embroidery silks. Grandma patted them lovingly. 'I don't need these now. I wondered if you would like them.'

Would she? Fanny could hardly contain herself. She didn't have any real interest in sewing at all but she could see that it would be a treasure trove for Clara Bones so she whispered 'Yes please,' and placed everything very carefully in a large orange Sainsbury's bag that her Grandma had found for her.

Inside a plastic container that her Grandad usually kept for storing his screws, Fanny found the slivers of soap that Grandma kept in a dish under the sink. Sometimes Grandma would place them in a pan of water and melt them down to make a mixture which, apparently, was very good for washing woollens in. She didn't mind, though, if Fanny used them to play with.. It seemed to gently amuse Grandma that Fanny could keep herself occupied with such unusual treasures.

Grandma seemed to think that this was a good time to have a clear out so after taking the two perfect apple crumbles out of the oven, she began to rifle through her other wooden drawers. Out came Grandad's old woollen socks which stopped fitting him when his bunions got worse. Out came six cotton shirts which stopped fitting him when he had been eating too much of Grandma's Yorkshire pudding and out came three pairs of woollen trousers which also had to be abandoned for the same reason as the shirts. 'You can have these as dressing up clothes, if you like Fanny!' her Grandma suggested, holding out a bin liner for Fanny to place her treasures into.

The next drawer held buttons, ribbons, silk lining and yards of beautiful lace. 'I don't think we'll make a seamstress out of you Fanny but you have a good imagination and I'm sure you'll be able to find something to do with these.'

'Thank you,' Fanny whispered. What treasures she had that disappeared into the black bin liner.

'Now let me think what else there is………….' Grandma appeared to be talking more to herself than Fanny now. She appeared to be in a world of her own at that point before she suddenly announced 'Ah! Of course, the attic! I forgot about the attic.'

Fanny loved the attic which you reached via some narrow winding steps once you had passed the guest bedroom that Fanny always slept in. The attic held rows and rows of gold- leaved books with pictures of children from long ago. Even the very young boys were dressed in cotton smocks until they were about seven and then they started wearing breeches. Fanny was always fascinated by the faces of the children in the books but she was even more interested in the huge trunk and the bags upon bags of items that Grandma had stored away. Grandma was a great hoarder and liked to keep things in case they came in useful, but every so often she would have a 'splurge' and Fanny would take home the results of Grandma's splurge.

'This'll keep you amused, Fanny,' Grandma said as she climbed the last of the narrow stairs up into the attic, pausing as she did so to catch her breath. 'You look around and see what you would like.' She pulled another two black bin liners out of her pocket and gave them to Fanny.

The first box that Fanny looked in contained tins and tins of shortbread made with real butter. Fanny recalled her Grandma once saying that people were always buying her shortbread for presents though that she didn't like it. 'It's what they always buy old people,' she had laughed. It appeared that she had stored it in the attic so that it didn't take over her scullery. At the bottom of the box of shortbread were some custard creams and pink wafers. Grandma liked to make her own biscuits so that she knew what was going into them. She wasn't keen on the sugary, puffy nonsense that were churned out by the factories. Fanny placed everything back into the box. She would ask Grandma if it was OK to take the box of biscuits as well as a couple of bags full of whatever she could find to fill them with. She remembered that when Grandma had asked her mother if she would like some biscuits, her mother had laughed, replying 'but what about my figure, Mabel?'

Another box revealed two tins of clotted cream fudge, some hand cream, some dried egg powder, six tins of 'Bully Beef' - which looked very old - and a large bag of dried milk powder, hiding two bars of Lifebuoy soap under it. The floor of the box was lined with some cotton vests. They still looked new.   There really was no point in emptying this box out either, since all the items could just remain inside.

By now, all the sights of the boxes and bags with all their contents flowing out was becoming too much for Fanny.

Everything was beginning to overwhelm her again, so she dragged the boxes to the little wooden guest bed and dived down under the eiderdown. Fanny did not particularly like the feel of the silkiness of the eiderdown, but the underside was cotton and she wrapped it around herself until she felt safe before drifting off to sleep and into the blackness.

Only Fanny did not find herself in bed. When she opened her eyes she found herself in Jack's house, surrounded by most of the boxes and bags that she had filled that day. Taking centre stage was her apple crumble, which stood on the table, still steaming gently and invitingly and surrounded by all the other food that Fanny had put to one side. And standing motionless, with her hands to her mouth - as though she had seen an apparition - was Clara Bones.

Chapter Eight

The fire sputtered and hissed in the long silence that followed. Clara Bones drew in a long breath as though she had somehow forgotten to breathe, spreading out her hands over all the treasures which Fanny had unwittingly brought with her.

'They're for you, Mrs Bones,' Fanny encouraged politely. 'My Grandma said that I could have them. I don't have light fingers. I just wanted to help.'

Mrs Bones opened one of the bags hesitatingly as though she couldn't take in everything without doing it slowly. The ribbon and lace fell out and lay nestled in the tiny bird-like hands of Mrs Bones. She held it gently, almost lovingly, stroking her finger across the material. She dipped into another bag before pulling out the shirts, trousers and socks that had belonged to Fanny's Grandad. Fanny knew that they were good quality. Her Grandma never bought anything less.

As Clara Bones dipped into each bag and box, Fanny took one of the tins of shortbread, prised it open and offered one of the buttered shortbreads to Jack's mother. Clara Bones took it between two fingers and bit into it delicately. A wonderful expression crossed her face as she did so. Fanny remembered a packet of wine gums that she had in her pocket and she pulled them out and laid them on the table. Still Mrs Bones hadn't said a word, but it appeared some thought was racing through her mind because she seemed to be concentrating very hard on it.

The blackness was beginning to descend again. Fanny could hear her Grandma's laboured steps as the stairs creaked under her weight.

'Why, Fanny, have you been asleep?' She looked at the two empty bin bags on the bed before glancing around the room. 'Well, it appears emptier, but it can't be. I'm sure my mind is playing tricks on me. Never mind, there's always tomorrow!'

Fanny nodded vigorously. She was looking forward to what the new day would bring when she delved into yet more boxes and bags. In fact, she couldn't wait. Somehow her normally uninteresting life had taken a different turn. She wondered what Jack would say when he saw all the treasures that she had managed to acquire for the family. She knew that she didn't have long to rifle through all the bags and boxes, for she had to go home at the weekend to clean her bedroom. Her mother was very particular about Fanny cleaning her bedroom, regardless of whether or not she had been at home and slept in her bed. It all seemed very peculiar to Fanny.

The following morning Fanny was up at five am. Daylight was streaming through the chink in the curtains, begging Fanny to get up. Fanny could hear her Grandparents moving around downstairs. They were always early risers.

'Early to bed and early to rise,

Makes a girl healthy, wealthy and wise' Fanny's Grandma would sing.

Fanny spooned down the thick creamy porridge, Grandma had prepared, capped with a heaped tablespoon of Gale's honey and a sprinkling of demerara to 'give it crunch.' She accepted the two slices of toast made with Hovis bread, spread thickly with Lurpak butter and homemade marmalade. Besides which, Grandma's toast was always tasty. Fanny then slipped a banana into her pocket 'for later.' Grandma would always insist on this, along with the fruit that nestled in the glass fruit bowl, and Grandad would always insist on giving Fanny a packet of sweets, also 'for later.'

'I'm going to look at the bags in the attic now, Grandma,' Fanny informed her Grandma as she swung her legs off the chair that Grandad had made.

'Will you be alright? Do you want any help?' Grandma asked, placing the empty porridge bowl in the sink.

'No, that's Ok! I'll manage,' Fanny shouted as she dashed up the stairs.

'That child is never still,' Grandad remarked. 'Just like a whirlwind.'

Grandma just nodded and continued to stack the sink with the breakfast things.

Fanny resolved to be more methodical. She would start at one end of the room and look carefully at each item before deciding whether it would be of use to the Bones family. The first two bags contained jigsaws and old newspapers. Fanny couldn't think of a use for them so she hauled the bags to one side and started on the next one, a red paper carrier bag with think twined thread for handles. It was rather a pretty bag.

Fanny was delighted to find some necklaces and bracelets, ring and lockets. Grandma had collected them over the years but didn't wear jewellery – only the thick golden wedding and ruby engagement ring - on her right 'wedding' finger. Grandma had been quite happy for Fanny to use the jewellery for 'dressing up', although Fanny was not a `dressing up' kind of girl. Further down inside the bag were some Christmas ornaments, cutlery, china cups and saucers wrapped up in soft paper and some gold-rimmed dinner- and side plates.

Fanny was surprised to find a whole box of jars of different flavoured jams. Grandma liked to make her own so it was not surprising it had been relegated to the attic. The box was very heavy, so Fanny tugged it to the bed and took some jars out until the box was light enough to pick up and place on the bed. Then she carefully put the jars back.

A huge but flatter box contained pristine cotton sheets, embroidered pillowcases, a double eiderdown, three hot water bottles and some knitted blankets. Fanny was very excited by this find but even more so when she found some heavy brocade curtains neatly folded, wrapped in plastic and bound with masking tape. Each bag and box she opened contained something that she felt sure Clara Bones would be able to make use of. Fanny's grandmother had been a tailoress and had stored boxes of materials and sewing items in the attic, no longer having any use for them. But neither did she want to throw them away.

Fanny kept dragging bags and boxes to the bed, being very careful to leave a space under the top of the eiderdown that she could crawl into and hope that she would be swept off to Jack's house. She hadn't seen Jack for a while. Even though he was very smelly and dirty and didn't say much, in a way he was still good fun.

The bed was now stacked with bags and boxes. Fanny had been delighted to find even more food, including tinned fruit in syrup and condensed milk. Grandma didn't hold with fruit in syrup nor with condensed milk. 'It rots your teeth,' she said, although even when Grandma had sent him to the shop with a list, Granddad always appeared to bring it back with him. The tinned peaches, golden plums, prunes, pears and condensed milk found a home on the top of the bed. Fanny was pleased that they had the ring-pull on the top of the can, but she didn't know if Victorians had tin openers.

Fanny climbed onto the bed and slid under the eiderdown, wrapping it firmly around her until only her nose and mouth were visible. She had to curl up tightly for there was very little room left for her. 'Jack, where are you?' she mouthed.

It didn't take long for the mist to descend and the blackness to momentarily envelope her. When Fanny opened her eyes all her bags and boxes were neatly piled on top of the table in the Bones' dwelling. Two small children were sitting on the bed, firstly looking wide-eyed at Fanny and then back at Clara Bones and Jack, who were both sitting near the fire. Reassured, the two younger children smiled at Fanny, whilst at the same time, Jack jumped up, smiling broadly. 'Hello, Fanny,' Jack greeted her. 'I was wondering when you would turn up.' He pointed at the smaller of the two boys, who was of fair complexion, with the same dimples that Maria and Robert had. 'This is Thomas, and this - said Jack pointing to a boy who was not unlike Jack with his dark, spiky hair - 'is William, but we call him Liam.'

Clara Bones motioned to the chair next to her. 'Please come and sit down. We wanted to thank you for all your gifts'. Clara picked up the garment she was working on. It was a pair of corduroy dungarees. 'This is Thomas's uniform for his new job as gardener's boy along with Liam at the Forbes household. It was a little long but with all the food you have given us I'm sure Thomas will grow soon.' Clara rummaged in the corner of the room, picking up the material that Fanny recognised as coming from her Grandma's house. 'Lady Forbes wants me to make her a dress with this. I'll get twelve shillings when it's finished.'

Jack let out a low whistle. This was obviously a lot of money.

'I sold some more clothing I made with the material you brought us – such fine quality material. I bought a sewing machine with the money. I'll be faster, although stitching flimsy material and setting in sleeves will still have to be done by hand.'

Jack had wandered over to the table, trying not to look too eager at the thought of what might be in the boxes and bags. Liam and Thomas were not so restrained and had already pulled the tape off the large flatter box to reveal the bedding.

'Oh!' they chorused in unison, their eyes widening in wonder. 'What's it for, Jack?' Thomas cried.

'What's it for?' Liam echoed.

Fanny was sitting on her hands, trying to restrain herself from getting up and showing the two youngsters how a bed was made in her time. She didn't think it would be polite, given that Clara Bones had wanted Fanny to sit beside her.

'Go on', Clara urged Fanny.

Fanny didn't need to be asked twice. She pulled the filthy, scratchy woollen blanket off the stained mattress, letting it drop to the floor. Then, walking slowly, she took two of the sheets out of the box, handing one to Jack to hold. Then, copying the method she had seen her Grandma employ, she shook the sheet until it unfolded.. It took Fanny a long time. She wasn't very tall and the sheet seemed very large. She spread it over the bed by climbing onto the mattress. By this time, Liam and Thomas had realised what Fanny was trying to achieve, so, after watching Fanny do it they smoothed the sheet out and tucked it in. Fanny wanted to put the pillowcases on next but she didn't have any pillows. She stood on one leg, and with her finger in her mouth, she pondered before rummaging through the bags until she found some material to stuff the pillowcases with. It would do for now, she thought. The boys were fascinated when the second sheet was shaken over the bed. They'd never had sheets, never mind two of them. The knitted blankets went on next before the eiderdown was spread out and the top sheet folded over the top of it, just as Fanny had seen her Grandma do.

'You need to fill these water bottles up with hot water,' Fanny said to Jack, handing him all three. Jack did as he was told, taking the water from a kettle sitting next to the fire. 'I'm not old enough to do it myself yet!' he muttered. She tested all the tops to make sure that Jack had tightened them enough before placing them in the bed. She didn't want them leaking all over the bed.

'Now jump in', she commanded the two younger boys, pointing at the bed. They didn't need to be asked twice. They tore off their breeches and shirts revealing long woollen underwear which they kept on as they piled into the bed.

A look of bliss flitted across their faces as the warmth cocooned their thin frames and a contented sigh escaped from them both. Thomas stuck his thumb in his mouth and sucked it like a baby. Very soon his eyes closed and he fell asleep. He looked very vulnerable, with his pale complexion and pinched cheeks. Liam did not look much stronger but he appeared more robust in some ways. His job as a gardener's boy had, at least, allowed him to be out into the fresh air, so his skin was tanned. Thomas had been inside the factory, cleaning the machines for sixteen hours a day. It was a good job that Mrs Forbes had found a position for him with Liam as a gardener's boy.

Clara and Jack were still opening the bags. Jack had found the box of jams and was inspecting each jar as though he couldn't quite believe what he was seeing. Clara had found the heavy brocade curtains and was holding them up above the door to see if one was long enough to keep the draft out. Satisfied that the curtains would cover the door and the windows she returned to the table and began to take out the tins of fruit and condensed milk which she stacked up in fours after carefully inspecting each one. The look on her face was a picture. Fanny had never experienced the delight of something so simple, giving as much pleasure as it was, to the Bones family.

When Jack found the cutlery, china cups and saucers and gold rimmed plates he turned to his mother and said, 'You'll be a lady now Clara Bones.'

A gentle snoring from the corner of the room alerted Fanny to the fact that Liam had now fallen asleep; one arm was wrapped protectively around Thomas, who was still sucking his thumb, and the other was firmly wrapped around the blue hot water bottle. They looked like the defenceless little lambs which Fanny had seen gambolling around the fields in early spring and were susceptible to bad weather and marauders. In the morning, they would no doubt find the wealth of goodies that had now been unpacked and were sitting on the table. Fanny had hoped to see their faces when they discovered all the fruit and jam, but that would have meant staying the night and there was only one bed. She liked the two little boys, Mrs Bones and Jack but she did not want to sleep in the bed with them and there was only one bed in which they all slept.

Mrs Bones began packing the food back into the boxes and sliding them under the bed. 'There's lots of thieves about around here,' she informed Fanny, 'It wouldn't do for the likes of them to know what goes on here.'

The fire was dying down, and glowing embers along with the occasional flicker of an escaping flame cast eerie shadows on the wall. Clara Bones had taken up the material she was working on and holding it very close to her face. It was getting too dark to continue, yet this was her livelihood and without the money it brought in she and the children would starve.

Jack had torn up some of the boxes which had contained the bedding and curtains, and was feeding the cardboard onto the fire, which responded by crackling into life. The shadows from the flames danced merrily on the walls as warmth emanated into the room once again. It was summer here and yet the sun's warmth did not penetrate these dank, dark dwellings with their weeping walls and fusty atmosphere. Only the flies - the carriers of summer diarrhoea - appeared to appreciate this pokey room. The stench still invaded London and this humble dwelling had not escaped the stink which permeated the air that Fanny breathed. Every time she visited Victorian London she noticed it only a little less. It still upset her and although she had taken to stuffing wads of cotton wool up her nostrils in an effort to lessen the stench, It hadn't really worked.

'What day is it here?' Fanny asked Clara Bones.

'Why, it's Sunday,' Clara responded, breaking off another piece of thread with her teeth. `Thomas starts his new job at the Forbes household tomorrow as a gardener's boy with Liam and if he does well, Liam will become groom. At least they are fed well and the uniform's free. It's our Jack I worry about now. Chimney sweeping is a dangerous job.'

Mrs Bones began to sing softly,

'Chimney sweeping's a dangerous job

And doesn't earn more than a couple of bob

Sweep! Sweep! Sweep!

Our lives aren't ours to keep

Children aren't worth a penny for ten

Get stuck, you'll ne'er be home again.'

'Time for bed,' Mrs Bones said, as she carefully folded the material she had been working on and laid it on the chair. Jack was already beginning to strip, just leaving his undergarments on. Fanny wasn't sure that Jack should be doing that when she was in the room, but it did not appear to worry him. He climbed carefully over Liam and Thomas before lying down. Mrs Bones was already beginning to undress, leaving her cotton bodice on. She turned to Fanny with a question in her expression.

'I'll just sit by the fire a bit longer,' Fanny told her. 'I'm not really tired.' The truth was that she was very tired but she didn't think she could share a bed with people that she hardly knew. She didn't even think she could share a bed

86

with people that she did know. It would be so much better sitting on the hard, uncomfortable chair and gazing at the dying embers until she was called back to her own time. It was all so very peculiar.

The warmth from the fire made Fanny's head droop with heaviness. She felt lethargic and her eyelids were beginning to close with fatigue. She jerked as she always did before sleep overtook her and momentarily opened her eyes. She was back in her Grandma's attic. She knew her Grandma must have been up to check on her because there was a hot cup of milky coffee and a digestive biscuit placed on the bedside cabinet for her.

Fanny could overhear her Grandma's voice floating up from the kitchen as she talked to her Granddad. 'I knew that child had gotten up too early. She's fast asleep again.'

Chapter Nine

The following day was Fanny's last day at her Grandparent's house, a last chance to rummage through the remaining plastic bags and boxes and - if she had time - to open the huge, heavy wooden trunk and see what treasures it held. Firstly though, Grandma wanted some help with the baking. Grandma liked making flapjack and Robin cake and gingerbread which, when it was baked and allowed to cool, was wrapped in buttered greaseproof and stored in tins on top of the scullery shelf.

Grandma was displeased that morning, although her displeasure was mild. Grandma had sent Granddad to the shop and he had founds tins of rice pudding which were 'on offer.'

'To think,' Grandma said, 'when I have been making *real* rice pudding all these years and he brings home some sloppy stuff.'

Fanny knew what Grandma meant, for Grandma's rice pudding was thick and creamy, with a skin on the top and plump sultanas lurking in its depth. Grandma always sprinkled her rice pudding with cinnamon for extra flavour. Tinned rice pudding wasn't a patch on Grandma's homemade pudding so she knew that Grandma was going to stack the tins on the bottom tread of the stairs ready to store in the attic. Fanny knew that if Grandma had offered them to Fanny's mother she would probably have taken them, but Grandma was a little fed up of the sort of ingratitude that Fanny's mother appeared to show when she was offered something.

Never mind, thought Fanny, feeling assured that Jack's family would enjoy the results of Grandad's shopping. And although Fanny kept hopping about, impatient to explore the attic's contents, Grandma was insistent that she show Fanny how to make a proper rice pudding. At last, the huge milky treat was ready to be placed in the oven and be baked 'to perfection' as Grandma always said it would be.

Fanny was free to go and she skipped through the kitchen, picking up a carrier bag on the way to carry all the tins of rice pudding in.

They were the first of her treasures to be placed on the bed. Another, a tall box taped up with shiny brown tape, was difficult for Fanny to open, but eventually she tore the tape off. The box was nearly as tall as she was and because she couldn't see what was inside, she tipped it over on its side and watched as coloured bricks and teddies and dolls in fine clothes and tiny cars in primary colours tumbled out. A smaller box inside this tall one contained plastic farm animals of all kinds and a 'build it yourself' farmhouse. Fanny had never seen Liam and Thomas play with toys, but she felt sure that they would like these once they had been transported to their home. Fanny divided the toys up into smaller boxes. She would never have managed to lift the huge box up onto the bed – not by herself anyway.

The treasures began to pile up on the bed in the attic. There was still plenty of material of all different textures and colours, wrapped up in different coloured tissue paper, as well as pots of pins and three pairs of dressmaking scissors. Fanny was especially pleased to find an artist's easel, a set of drawing pencils, three large pads of superior drawing paper, and tubes of paint, brushes and a great many pastel crayons. Fanny knew Jack could draw. She had seen the drawing he had done of the family that he lost in a cholera outbreak. When he had put pencil to paper, the marks he made had brought to life a family that Fanny could never meet. There had been a small batch of drawing paper and some pencils in the last lot of stuff that Fanny had taken with her, but this consignment contained much, much more. I wonder who used to draw, Fanny mused to herself.

Many of the boxes contained old books which didn't seem appropriate to send to Victorian England. None of the boys could read or write and Fanny was fairly certain that Mrs Bones couldn't either. Perhaps, though, she could teach them. Fanny was an excellent reader and story writer: gifts which her teacher had suggested were partly due to her overactive imagination. Fanny didn't mind having an overactive imagination. She liked reading and she liked writing stories and she would use this to help the

Bones family learn to read and write. She scattered around the room those boxes that contained items she didn't think could be of some use. Fanny didn't want Grandma to be suspicious and ask where everything had gone since it was quite obvious that Fanny hadn't taken anything downstairs. Luckily, Grandma could be quite absentminded and had probably forgotten most of the things that the attic had stored. It was quite likely that she had already forgotten about the rice pudding and Granddad would not dare mention it. He had been in enough trouble as it was when he had brought the tins home.

Fanny really wanted to lift open the great heavy lid of the trunk, but some framed drawings piled up in the very corner of the room caught her eye. They were pictures of scenes that Fanny had become very familiar with, for they captured the heart of the Victorian slum dwellings, the narrow cobbled streets, the pinched features of the waifs lying shoeless in the gutters with pleading, desperate eyes. The pictures would be a reminder forever of the terrible lives of the Victorian Poor. A tear rolled down Fanny's cheek. How different her life was. She picked up one of the pictures and stumbled downstairs. Grandma was just taking the rice pudding out of the oven.

'What have you got there?' Grandma enquired, as she laid the huge baking dish on the top of the cooker.

Fanny held out the dusty black and white picture for Grandma to take off her. Grandma paused before touching the picture, as though it was the most precious thing in the whole world. 'I'd forgotten that I'd got these. `This, Fanny, is Victorian England.'

'I know,' said Fanny, wiping the dust off her fingers onto her dress.

Grandma wasn't listening to Fanny. 'When I was a little girl, an old gentleman drew these and gave them to me. They were my prized possessions for a long time although I didn't really understand what they represented. I was born in later Victorian times and things were very much better than they were In early Victorian times. I think this was drawn in 1854, just weeks before the Great Cholera Epidemic which started in Soho. So many people lost their lives before they realised what was causing it. They should have boiled the water.' Grandma paused, as though thinking deeply. 'There should be a picture of me up there that the gentleman drew when I was about your age.'

'I'll go and look for it, Fanny promised, I'll do that right now!'

Fanny scuttled off. Her Grandma had kept the black and white picture of the narrow back-to-back terraced houses and had propped it up at the back of the kitchen working surface. Fanny wouldn't be surprised if Grandad was asked to knock a picture hook into the wall to hang it up on. No, she wouldn't be surprised at all.

It did not take Fanny long to find the picture of Grandma as a little girl, for she looked so much like Fanny herself that it was uncanny. Grandma was about eight and was standing in a stream with her skirts lifted up and her tawny hair tumbling in waves down her back. Her eyes were startling blue like Fanny's and she had the same dreamy look that Fanny's mother often complained that Fanny had. Really, Grandma had been quite beautiful.

Fanny hurried downstairs with her treasure, wiping her dusty fingers on the wallpaper on the way down because she did not like the feel of dust or pastel crayons or chalk. These sensations made her cringe. Fanny handed the picture to her Grandmother. 'You were very beautiful, Grandma,' Fanny cried.

'So are you.' Her Grandma said, stroking Fanny's hair gently, 'So are you.'

Grandma allowed Fanny to sleep in the attic for her last night's stay. She normally tucked Fanny into bed but her 'old bones were creaking' and because Granddad was still out working on the car, it was left to Fanny to put herself to bed. Fanny was pleased about this as she didn't know how she was going to explain to her Grandma why the bed was stacked up with all manner of things – including the rice pudding.

It was not long after she had slid under the eiderdown that she found herself back in Jack's house with all the boxes of goods piled up in their usual fashion on the table.

Jack saw her first, but Fanny had to take another look to make sure it was him. He looked clean and he didn't smell quite so bad, although the stench of London's sewage problem was still very evident all around her. Jack's normally spiky hair, normally blackened and stiffened with grime and soot, was now golden and wavy, as was Thomas's - and likewise as Maria and Robert's had been before the cholera had taken them. Fanny also noticed that Jack's breeches were made of the warm woollen material that her Granddad's Sunday trousers had been made from and that his shirt was of the very best cotton, and had been cut down and reshaped from her Grandad's Sunday best. Jack looked quite handsome.

'Why Jack, you're so clean!' Fanny exclaimed, unable to help herself.

Jack grinned. It wasn't often that Fanny had seen Jack without his serious expression, so she wasn't so sure how to react.

'I'm a sweep no more,' Jack explained. 'Good riddance and all that. Jack Bones at your service, Ma'am!'

Fanny didn't know what he meant, so she did what she did best and stuck her finger in her mouth whilst waiting for Jack to continue.

Jack stuck his fingers under his armpits. 'I'm a trader now,' he informed her. `I sell the garments me Ma makes and the jewellery you brought with you, door to door and,' he said with a flourish, 'I sold one of me paintings to Charles Dickens!'

'Charles Dickens!' exclaimed Fanny, 'Who's he?'

'A great social reformer and writer,' Jack explained, 'author of A Christmas Carol and The Pickwick Papers and................ others,' he finished lamely. 'He's trying to change things for the poor. One and sixpence, he paid me .... Just think, one and sixpence for a drawing!'

'What was Charles Dickens like?' Fanny asked.

Jack thought for a moment. 'He had a kind face and a short beard. I dunno really, I was too shocked when he stopped and asked to look at what I was drawing.'

Jack, it transpired, had taken to drawing on his travels to the doors of the richer inhabitants of London, as he plied his trade. He would stop when something caught his eye and, taking his pencil, would bring a scene to life. Then he would continue on his way, door to door, with the fine garments his mother had made. He had drawn pictures of the little girl with the phossie jaw but kept them hidden in the back of the pad. The rich didn't want a reminder of the grim realities of the Industrial Revolution but, instead, they bought the pictures of the vases of flowers that Jack drew, especially after hearing that Charles Dickens had been a customer of Jack's.

'Shall we go out, Fanny?' Jack implored her, 'and leave Ma to open what you've brought?'

Fanny wasn't sure about this, for she hadn't really enjoyed the experience last time, but, having tucked the pad of paper under his arm, a couple of pencils into his pocket, he dashed out of the door, leaving no time for Fanny to express her opinion.

Again they weaved in and out of the narrow, blackened streets of London, where the washing flapped aggressively above them and thick black smoke belched overhead. Yet the little girl with the phossie jaw had gone. 'She died.' Jack explained, 'nothing but the pauper's grave for her.'

He scurried up the back streets until they opened out into wider streets which Fanny hadn't seen before. There were rows of shops but many of them did not sell anything that Fanny had seen in the shops of the time that she lived in. For instance, one large shop proudly displayed the sign 'Gun Merchants' as though it was the most normal thing to sell guns to the public.

Next door was a leech merchant who only sold the blood-sucking creatures whose job it was to suck out any bad blood causing disease. Fanny wrinkled her nose in disgust.

'It's germs, Jack,' she cried, `It's germs that cause disease. Leeches won't cure you.'

Jack, though, didn't understand, and not knowing what to say, he carried on walking briskly so that Fanny had to run to keep up with him. They scurried on past the butcher's and grocer's and the milliner's that sold hats for the rich. On they went past the tripe-dressers who sold the stomach of animals, a delicacy in Victorian times. Her Grandma had once bought some for Granddad, who was particularly fond of tripe. It was white and rubbery and smelt like fish that had gone off. Fanny had refused to try it even though Grandad had sprinkled it liberally with vinegar and declared it very tasty. As the shops gave way to a less busy area, a tall- spired church loomed upon them, its graveyard dotted with tombstones. Jack took out his pad, and, stooping to enter the archway that fronted the graveyard, he sat on a stone and began to draw. He pointed some distance away. 'Those are pauper's graves. That's where me Da, Robert, Maria and the twins are. Sometimes there's fifteen or more in a grave. Last week, Mr Gaukrodger the gravedigger was overcome by the fumes, fell in and died. He were only twenty three.'

Fanny plonked herself down on the tombstone beside Jack. She didn't know if this would be allowed in her time but it was a seat on which to sit until Jack had finished scribbling. She hoped that he wasn't going to draw all the tombstones, because they stretched as far as the eye could see. She leaned against Jack so that she could get closer and see how far he had got. He had sketched in the area of the graveyard, but instead of tombstones he had drawn daisies and buttercups and trees with slim trunks spreading their limbs out to provide shelter for whoever walked by. Maria's face peeped out from behind the birch and Robert was running through the grass, laughing, with his tangled locks of hair blowing in the breeze. Jack rarely spoke of the siblings who had died from the cholera or of his Da who was the first to die, but it was clear that he hadn't forgotten them.

Jack tapped his paper with his pencil. 'That's enough for today.' He stretched his legs before standing up, ruffling his hair with his free hand. 'Ma should have finished the shirts by now and I need to sell them. She's plenty more material but there'll be a time when she'll have to buy some herself. Lady Forbes showed an interest in the one or two of the dresses for her two daughters as well. She liked that the material was unique as well as good quality and me Ma's a good seamstress. The Head Gardener – he's ordered a shirt – Sunday best – for when he goes to church.'

Fanny was finding it hard to keep up with Jack, whose legs seemed to have grown much longer recently, but she was also finding it difficult to keep up with all the changes in Jack's life. All these unwanted items in Grandma's attic had made a tremendous difference to Jack's family. He was even wearing an old pair of Grandad's shoes whilst Fanny was still trying to run barefoot, listen to Jack and dodge anything nasty that might be lurking on the cobbles. She must remember to put an old pair of shoes in the next bundles that would end up with the Bones family. That way, at least, she would not have to run again bare-footed through the cobbled streets of London.

Clara Bones had un-wrapped all the boxes by the time that Fanny and Jack returned to the dwelling. She was always quietly grateful and would return to inspect each item again and again as though not quite believing her good fortune. She had, indeed, finished the garments as she had promised. She had wrapped each garment in different coloured tissue paper. Two of the shirts were to go to the clothing shop which sold high-end goods but others would be sold door-to- door in the richer end of London. The dresses for the Forbes girls and the shirt for the Head Gardener had been packed in two separate boxes, awaiting delivery.

`Will you wait with me while Jack delivers these? Clara

Bones asked, pointing to the garments. 'I'll make a cup of tea, if you like.'

'I'll stay if you want me to, and keep you company,' Fanny replied, 'but I don't want a drink, thank you.' Fanny was thinking that the water wasn't too clean and furthermore, if she did have a drink she might have to use that awful privy.

Jack stretched himself out to his full height. '1853's a good year, I think.'

Fanny remembered a conversation that she'd had with her Grandma. 'Jack, listen! You must boil your water, you must get away. 1854 is going to be a bad year for the cholera and many people are going to die.' Fanny was struggling to say something else but the words were getting stuck in her head and the blackness was closing in. When she woke up she was back in the attic, tucked up in bed. The sun had just woken up and was sending pale golden rays onto Fanny's pillow through the chinks in the curtains. She lay there, wrapping the eiderdown even more tightly around her when, like then, she felt anxious. She lay like this for an hour, hoping and praying that Jack would have understood what she was trying to say. There were thoughts whirling around her head but she had to get up and pack her pink suitcase ready to go home. She hadn't had time to push the lid of the heavy trunk open and she had to be washed and dressed and presentable for her mother by 10am. Fanny could smell breakfast wafting up the stairs. She dressed quickly, scrubbed her face and hands in the bathroom one floor down, and took her place at the breakfast table.

The plate of bacon and fried egg topped with plum tomatoes and fingers of toast helped calm Fanny.

Grandma knew what she liked, and sitting in the warmth of Grandma's kitchen amongst all the activities of normality that described this place had a calming effect on Fanny.

Fanny had eaten most of the bacon and the yolk of the egg before she carefully put down her knife and fork and asked, 'What was the cholera epidemic of 1854 like?' She did not like the white of the egg and had pushed it to one side of her plate.

Fanny seemed to think that her Grandma could answer her every question, but instead of answering immediately, her Grandma disappeared into the parlour and came back with a huge gold-leaved book entitled 'The Life and Times of the Victorians.' The cover was not very exciting and it smelt musty - of times long ago - as though bringing some of that era into the present.

Grandma opened the book carefully. 'The Broad Street cholera outbreak in Soho killed 616 people.' she began. Fanny nodded. She knew where Broad Street was because it was near Jack's house. She had passed through it when exploring the streets with Jack.

'It started on August 31st 1854 and within one day seventy people had died. Only one week later, 400 people had died altogether. Everyone thought the cause was the 'miasma' or bad smell in the atmosphere. Even Florence

Nightingale, who was a very famous nurse, thought that cholera was due to the miasma.

A man called Dr Jon Snow did not think so. He thought that the disease was spread by contaminated water and he persuaded the authorities to remove the handle from the water pump on September 8th. The deaths from cholera dropped almost immediately. Dr Jon Snow was now convinced that he had enough evidence to show that the cause of cholera was not the stink of London but a water-borne disease. Dr Snow presented this to the St James Parish Vestry, which was responsible for the health of those who lived in Soho. He was helped by the Reverend Henry Whitehead, but the people in higher authority couldn't get it out of their heads that it was the miasma that caused cholera They wouldn't listen to the findings of Dr John Snow or Reverend Whitehead, even though many lives had been saved.'

Grandma traced her finger down the page. 'Oh yes, there was another outbreak of cholera which was spread by contaminated water in the slums. That occurred in the East End of London and even more people died then than did in the 1854 outbreak. It was a bad business, a bad business ……..'

'When did cholera first begin?' Fanny asked her Grandma. By now Fanny had finished her plate and was helping herself to a doorstep which she was liberally spreading with Grandma' homemade lemon cheese.

'It began in Sunderland in October 1831. A ship carrying sailors stricken with the disease docked at the port. The Government wanted all the ships from the Baltic States to be isolated, but the port authorities simply ignored the Government. The disease travelled throughout Scotland and down to London. It reached London in 1832 and by the time cholera had finished its course it had taken 52,000 lives.'

'52,000,' Fanny exclaimed. It was too huge a number to even contemplate.

'Germs weren't discovered until 1864, so no one really knew how to prevent or treat cholera, even though Dr Jon Snow had proved that something in the water was causing it. When the doctors had first mistakenly thought disease was carried by smell, houses had to be lime washed and barrels of tar and vinegar were burned in the streets. This was all done to try and get rid of the bad smell but, of course, none of this worked. Still, cholera did not kill anywhere near the numbers of people that TB did.'

Fanny was about to open her mouth and ask what TB was, but just as she was about to spread another doorstep with lemon cheese, there was a knock on the door that preceded her mother walking in.

'Are you ready, Fanny?' her mother demanded. 'it's time to go home now!'

'Let the child finish her breakfast,' Grandma implored, as Fanny sucked the lemon cheese off her fingers slowly and delicately.

'Hmpph!' Fanny's mother snorted. 'Still eating breakfast at 10am. What is the world coming to and what *will* you be teaching her next. Go on then, hurry up while I'm stacking this suitcase in the boot.'

'There's a couple of bags of treasures that Fanny's taking home, which she found in the attic,' Grandma informed Fanny's mother.

'Not more rubbish to fill up her bedroom, surely?' Fanny's mother replied abruptly, before picking up the suitcase and two black bin liners. `I don't know why I bother, I really don't!' She marched off.

Fanny was going to ask her mother what she was bothered about but decided against it. She was already in enough trouble for enjoying her breakfast at an unsuitable time and the fact that some lemon cheese had fallen and smeared her dress wouldn't go down well. It would just mean more washing for her mother.

Fanny's mother noticed the picture of Grandma hanging on the wall when she returned from placing the luggage and bin liners in the car- boot. 'Who's that?' she enquired, 'It looks an awful lot like Fanny, but it can't be, dressed in clothes like that.'

She peered at the picture intently.

Fanny was hopping up and down on one foot with excitement. 'It's Grandma,' she announced excitedly. `She looked like me when she was a little girl. An old gentleman drew her when she was about my age.'

'An old gentleman?' Her mother frowned. 'And who might that be, Mabel?' She scraped the glass of the frame, breathed on it and polished it with a paper hankie which she withdrew from her pocket.

Grandma was frowning with concentration, her hand pressed firmly to the side of her cheek as though that would somehow help her remember. Grandma's memory hadn't been too good since she'd had a bout of pneumonia last year.

'There's a name here,' Fanny's mother announced triumphantly, `but it's very faint. I can make out a J and a B though. John? Jeremy? Jaden? Jacob?'

'None of those names sounds familiar', Grandma replied, still frowning hard with the effort of trying to remember. `It's hard remembering names nowadays.'

Fanny's mother took her daughter by the hand and tugged her towards the door. 'Thank you for looking after Fanny,' she said politely, 'Fanny, where are your manners?'

'Thank you for having me, Grandma,' Fanny shouted, as she disappeared down the garden path, past the privy, out of the gate and toward the car. She could see her Grandma waving at her.   Grandma was mouthing something that Fanny couldn't hear.   Then the breeze caught Grandma's words and carried them along faintly towards Fanny …..'I remembered the name of the man who drew all those pictures. He was a gentleman called Jack Bones. 'Yes, that's right, his name was Jack Bones.'

ISBN 978-1-912505-13-5

9 781912 505135 >

www.ingramcontent.com/pod-product-compliance
Lightning Source LLC
Chambersburg PA
CBHW030551130626
46552CB00006B/2505